One Last Breath

A Look Back at 200 Years of Global Warming

Written by John Coviello

Edited by Gary Arnold

ISBN: 9798653242663

ROK Enterprises Publishing

One Last Breath, A Look Back at 200 Years of Global Warming

Copyright © 2020 by John Coviello

Contents

List of Figures

Forward

This novella is meant to be a wake-up call and a call to action. Rachel Carson's book "Silent Spring" galvanized prior generations to take actions to protect the environment, which culminated in the first Earth Day on April 22, 1970 and the passing of numerous sensible environmental laws that have improved the environment and quality of life in many countries. In the spirit of Rachel Carson, this novella is intended to educate and galvanize current generations to take measures to address the potentially serious problem of ongoing global warming before it becomes unstoppable runaway global warming.

Chapter 1
Survivalism and Skepticism

Scott woke up late, looked over at his clock and noticed it was still dark outside. He loved this time of the year between Christmas and New Year's because it meant his dad was home for a week and his mom had time off from work. It was a rare stretch of family time that he sincerely cherished. It also happened to be when he had his birthday, having just turned eight the day before, which meant his parents threw him a birthday party in which he got to see the few friends and relatives that lived in the remote part of northern Canada in which he lived. It was truly his favorite week of the entire year.

His mom heard him rustling in his bedroom and called out, "Good morning Scott. I've got some hot pancakes and chocolate milk for you."

"Mmmm," Scott thought to himself as his mouth watered and his stomach growled. He loved when his mom was off from work and had time to make him pancakes.

As he ate his breakfast and intermittently chatted with his mom, his dad and grandfather (papa Joe) carried on a conversation.

"We'll be crazy busy this year with this government contract," his dad said excitedly. As much as he loved being with his family for a whole uninterrupted week, Scott's dad also loved having plenty of work to look forward to over the coming year. He worked as the foreman for a telecom company line installation crew, which meant he spent much of his time away from home as he traversed Canada overseeing installation projects.

"What's it about?" papa Joe asked.

"You know how the tundra has thawed in parts? Well, it's having a major impact on communication lines in communities and government installations in northern Canada," he told papa Joe with an air of excitement. "That means a lot of work for my crew!" he said with a grin.

"That's great son! I'm happy for you and your crew! But it's another thing the climate agitators will jump on to shut down our oil tar sands operations and that's bad for Canada. They'll jump on anything to push their green agenda. It's as if they never knew the world has naturally warmed up many times in the past before we were around," papa Joe said with conviction.

His dad's eyes lit up as papa Joe's response stirred a memory, "You wouldn't believe what I saw at a site last summer in the northern region of Ontario! We had to dig down several meters to extend a buried line and we hit a bunch of fossilized palm tree branches, and a crocodile jaw fossil. I've read about Earth being warm and ice-free millions of years ago with palm trees and crocodiles in what are now cold northern parts, but to actually observe these tropical plants and a remnant of a crocodile firsthand; I've got to tell you it was something to see! Such a strange sight in such a cold place. It makes me wonder if you are onto something papa with your skepticism about us causing global warming."

Papa Joe responded with a smile, "I might be old, but I'm no fool. There is a whole industry that has developed around studying why the Earth is warming and some people are living quite well from it, while many of us know this has happened naturally in the past."

Having only turned eight years old yesterday, Scott soaked in his dad and papa's conversation, as he sat eating his breakfast. Like most kids his age, he was more concerned with watching cartoons and playing video games online than thinking much about things like Earth's climate and how or why it was changing. But since he didn't have much else to focus on when his mom had stopped talking, he focused his attention on his dad and papa's conversation. One of many they had in front of him questioning whether global warming was natural or caused by mankind.

While Scott's dad was out across Canada working, which was a good part of the year, papa Joe spent a lot of time raising him when his mom was busy working or had things to do. He saw it as his duty to raise his grandson as an outdoorsman. Given the remote location where they lived, learning how to endure the sometimes-harsh conditions outdoors was not some kind of luxury or hobby, it was a necessity for survival at various points in one's life. Living in the sparsely populated and remote areas of the Yukon, a person needed to know how to survive in the woods and live off the natural world.

It was during the long hours they spent outdoors that papa Joe let Scott know his views about global warming. How it could all be explained as natural processes that Earth had undergone many times in the past. That there was a conspiracy by environmentalists and scientists that were seeking control over people and funding to bolster their bank accounts by blaming the warming on mankind. Being a young and impressionable person, Scott took his papa's words at face value without questioning what he was being told. He looked up to his grandfather and trusted what he said as words of wisdom.

When he had time to play with kids close to his age, his friends echoed his grandfather's views, as papa's views seemed to be what most adults shared in their remote part of the world. This reinforced the notion in young Scott that his grandfather must be right about such things.

Chapter 2
Shifting Views

With the help of his grandfather, Scott grew to be a very resourceful teenager with a lot of knowledge and skills concerning how to survive in the wilderness. His mom was an avid reader and encouraged her son to read to learn about the world beyond them, which he gladly did since living in a remote area there were times when he didn't have much to do and had a keen intellect that soaked up a good book.

One of his favorite things to do with his mom was to join her on her semi-annual trip to Whitehorse, which is the only city in the Yukon. His mom liked to make the trip to break the monotony of living in a remote area and to do some browsing and shopping in stores, as they relied on parcel deliveries and one tiny local store that only carried basics. The semi-annual trips were a chance for her to try clothes on, see the latest gadgets firsthand, and just browse what the big stores offered. It was a real treat after spending months in the wilderness. It was also a chance for her to spend some quality time with her son.

Scott would take some money he saved up by selling birch syrup he produced from trees near his home and would use it to buy things like clothes, models of famous buildings that he enjoyed building with papa Joe in the shed behind their house, and sometimes electronic gadgets.

Scott's mom always made sure they stopped by a second-hand bookstore in Whitehorse that had a huge supply of used books that were inexpensive. This was a part of the trip that Scott also enjoyed a lot since he would randomly find books to read by leafing through the store's shelves. He found it fun looking through the books not knowing what he'd discover. It was a spontaneous shopping experience that was scarce in his era; a time in which shopping mainly entailed searching for what you wanted on the Internet with few surprises.

On a trip to Whitehorse when he was thirteen, in the summer of 2046, he randomly came across a book called, "A Time for Action for Future Generations" by the legendary climate change activist from Sweden, Greta Thunberg.

He had heard of Greta since she had won the *Time Person of the Year* award in 2019 and made her mark on history as a leading advocate for addressing climate change, but had no interest in reading any of her highly-acclaimed books about how to address the so-called climate crisis. In his worldview, which was strongly influenced by his grandfather, there was no climate crisis and Greta was just another one of those opportunistic people who had gained fame and fortune by dedicating her life to warning the world of a "crisis" that he did not believe was real and was not concerned about. Yes, he understood the world was warming, but he had been led to believe that it was due to natural causes and there was nothing to worry about.

After giving it a quick look, Scott was about to put her book back on the shelf when his curiosity compelled him to read the summary on the back cover. After reading the summary, he was intrigued and felt the need to hear another point of view about what was going on with the climate and bought her book. "It will be kind of interesting to hear the other side's point of view," he thought as he laid down five loonies for the book. Although much of the world had moved only to electronic payments, it was still common in remote areas like the Yukon for people to use cash to buy things.

Before they hit the road, there was one more stop to make. Since Scott had to endure hours of his mom browsing and shopping in stores, she made an agreement with him to stop at the "vircade" every time they visited Whitehorse. Video games had evolved into virtual reality (VR) games and the term "arcade" became a relic of a bygone era. This was another part of the trip that he enjoyed for the spontaneous experience of trying the latest

VR games. This time there was a new game called "Climate Crash" that was all the rage, as there were a bunch of kids waiting for their turn to play.

As soon as he put the VR goggles on, he found himself in a highly sophisticated control room as Director of the Climate Emergency Response Force, in charge of coordinating the world-wide response to the ongoing climate catastrophe. The game was fast-paced and thrilling. He had to make critical decisions as the months and years ticked by and carbon dioxide and global temperatures increased. He was faced with pressing decisions, such as whether to plant a massive number of trees in a specific area or whether to use man-made engineering methods to dim sunlight reaching the Earth and how much to dim it. The outcome was randomized, as sometimes the climate changed in unexpected ways and not all solutions worked out the same way during every game, with a world climate either stabilized or one careening out of control. Points were awarded for making correct decisions along the way, with a large bonus if the climate crisis was averted.

The graphics and three-dimensional experience were so lifelike that by the time the game was over, his heart was racing, and he was sweating as he felt adrenaline flowing through his body. When he took the goggles off, his head was spinning as he thought back to the virtual climate catastrophe he'd just prevented.

It was a warm July day in the Yukon as he and his mother made the long drive to their home a few hours north of Whitehorse. In fact, the radio said it was expected to be a record warm day and people should avoid driving on the normally frozen roads through the tundra, as they were melting and becoming muddy and unstable. Luckily, they weren't driving that far north.

He let the fresh warm Yukon air waft over his body as his mom drove with the SUV's windows down. Looking for something to do, he picked up Greta's book about the climate crisis and began to read it. His interest had been even more piqued after his virtual reality experience. He was so engrossed in the book he didn't realize the SUV had stopped until his mom said, "Let's get some lunch."

As they sat down for lunch, she smiled and said, "You must really like that book. I didn't hear a peep out of you for two hours."

Scott's head was spinning as he sat across from his mom. It wasn't just any old book that he had become enthralled with reading; it was a book that completely rocked his worldview he had developed throughout his youth. He was so taken aback by what he had read that he couldn't immediately put together a reply to her.

She could sense that he had been deeply affected by the book and asked, "Isn't that book by the Swedish Prime Minister Greta Thunberg, who led the campaign to raise awareness about climate change since she was a teenager?"

After drinking a sip of water and taking two deep breaths, Scott was finally able to get his head around what he had just read and replied, "Yeah, I didn't understand how much actual science is behind the predictions that the world will warm to dangerous levels and that there is very strong evidence that this warming is being caused by us. Greta really has a way with words and does a breathtaking job explaining climate change with citations to scientific papers and other supporting evidence. I was really blown away. I am kind of stunned, actually."

Scott's mom smiled a bit and replied, "I can see that."

Unlike his grandfather, Scott's mom took an interest in learning about global warming and was concerned about what it was doing to the planet, even in her remote part of the world that had so far escaped the worst impacts. She knew this day would come eventually and thought it was best to let Scott recognize the truth on his own rather than causing friction with papa Joe by trying to steer him in a different direction than his grandfather.

With a look of wonderment that only a child learning about something entirely new to him could have, Scott asked, "What do you think Mom? Will it be as bad as Greta says it will be?"

She replied, "Nobody really knows how bad it will get Scott. There is still some uncertainty regarding how much the planet will warm and if we can find a solution. As you know, even now that the Earth is feeling real impacts, there are those that deny it is even a problem."

Scott smiled, thinking of his grandfather and so many others back home who were more willing to believe wild conspiracy theories about climate change put forward by Internet cranks than hard scientific evidence provided by highly educated scientists.

His mom continued, "How bad it gets will depend upon choices we make soon and whether we can find a technological way out of this dilemma."

"What do you mean mom?" Scott demanded with a sincere look of concern.

A bit startled by his tone and genuine concern, she replied, "I mean we can choose a path where we ignore the science and ignore the mounting evidence and just take our chances with the future or we can use our brightest minds to make our best effort to power our lives without burning fossil fuels. The problem is we've already put so much carbon dioxide into the atmosphere that we've ensured the Earth will continue to warm even if we stop using fossil fuels tomorrow. I've read about research into technologies that would cool the Earth, such as massive machines that could remove carbon dioxide from the atmosphere and giant mirrors that could reflect the Sun's energy back into space before it hits our atmosphere. But, getting a worldwide consensus to build such massive things seems unlikely given many people's inability to be realistic about what the future climate may have in store for us and our inability to agree on much of anything."

Scott felt reassured by his mom's response that there were solutions to the climate crisis. He hadn't gotten that far into Greta's book yet.

Thinking about what Greta said about raising cattle and meat consumption being contributors to global warming, Scott pushed his half-eaten hamburger aside and said, "Let's get going. I want to read more."

As their SUV hummed along the lonely Yukon highway, he read for a good part of the trip, but wound up eventually putting the book down and fell into deep thought as he gazed at the beautiful scenery. His worldview that had been instilled in him by papa Joe had been shaken to its core and he had a lot of thinking to do about it. He literally felt like a different person versus the one who made the trip down to Whitehorse the prior morning.

His mom sensed that he was feeling conflicted and said, "papa Joe is a wonderful person who has done so much to help raise you. He has prepared you well to deal with the life ahead of you. Just keep in mind that he is of another generation that included many that were skeptical about claims that we are causing global warming. He genuinely believes what he taught you, as do many of his generation. There was some doubt, even in the scientific community, about whether global warming was caused by mankind when he was a younger man. The doubt was amplified by well-funded and sophisticated fossil fuel industry public relations campaigns designed to cast doubt on what climate scientists had to say about our role in causing global warming. It seems silly now that the Earth is warming far faster than it ever did naturally in the past, but that's what molded your grandfather's view of things."

Scott sighed and said, "I know he means well, mom. I don't have any hard feelings towards papa Joe. I just know that it will be my generation and those after us that will have to deal with this serious problem. All his ranting and raving about grand conspiracies and greedy scientists will not amount to a hill of beans in the long run as we young people have to deal with the reality of global warming. My generation and those that follow have a big mess to clean up."

Scott stared out of the window at the passing Yukon scenery the rest of the way home, thinking about what he had read. He smiled as they passed four young black bear cubs playfully wrestling in grass by the side of the road as their mom watched over them. As the SUV reached a crest in the road revealing the beauty of the Yukon countryside, he thought, "This beauty never gets old." His mom smiled, as she understood why he was deep in thought and knew that his life would never be the same.

Chapter 3

Roots of Climate Change Research

Scott spent his teenage years honing his outdoors skills with his grandfather. After his fateful trip to Whitehorse with his mom, he took it upon himself to learn all he could about global warming and how the climate was changing. It became an avid interest of his he pursued during his spare time, which he kept secret from his grandfather.

One of the things he was surprised to learn was just how far back the science of studying climate change went. It was not something that emerged in the 21st century or even the 20th century. Its origins went all the way back to the 19th century, during a time when scientists were trying to figure out what caused the Earth to experience ice ages. It was also a time when quickly industrializing human societies started emitting greenhouse gases into the atmosphere in significant quantities.

In a paper published in 1824, a French mathematician and physicist named Joseph Fourier made a hypothesis that gases in the Earth's atmosphere create a barrier that prevents heat from escaping. Prophetically, he predicted in a paper that appeared in 1837 in the American Journal of Science and Arts that over a long time period both natural causes and human activities could cause the heat in the atmosphere to change.

There was no experimental evidence supporting Fourier's hypothesis that gases within the Earth's atmosphere could heat the atmosphere until a little-known amateur scientist from the United States named Eunice Newton Foote performed experiments during the 1850s that tested Fourier's hypothesis. She found that jars filled with humid air that mimicked water vapor and jars filled with carbon dioxide were hotter than ones filled with dry air when all three types of jars were exposed to the sun.

Being a woman scientist at that time, she was not allowed to present her research findings during an 1856 conference at the American Association for the Advancement of Science. Her findings had to be read into the record by a male colleague. This obscured her important contribution to climate science.

Her work was not widely known when an Irish scientist named John Tyndall set out in 1859 to perform similar experiments with more precise instruments. He wanted to figure out which atmospheric gases could hold or lose heat; a finding that he hoped might explain the cause of past ice ages. He replicated Eunice Newton Foote's findings that both carbon dioxide and water vapor trapped heat much more effectively than dry air. In fact, he was astonished to find that carbon dioxide trapped as much as one thousand times more heat than dry air.

These findings changed scientists' understanding of the heat trapping capabilities of carbon dioxide and water vapor and their role in heating up the Earth's atmosphere. A critical role that maintains Earth's temperature at a level that is warm enough to sustain life. Scientists performing such investigations during the middle of the 19th century could hardly imagine the problems humans would face just two centuries later, as too much of a good thing in the form of heat trapping atmospheric gases threatened to overheat the planet and cause massive environmental damage to all living things on Earth, including mankind.

The first glimpse by a scientist into the potential for human-caused climate change resulted from an ambitious effort by a Swedish physicist named Svante Arrhenius. He was driven by a desire to show how much carbon dioxide is needed in the atmosphere to change global temperatures. He did this to support his hypothesis that changes in the atmosphere, such as changes in heat trapping gases including carbon dioxide, was the best explanation regarding why ice ages occurred in the past.

Arrhenius used recently released data from Swedish geologist Arvid Högbom that included an estimate regarding how much carbon dioxide was present in the Earth's atmosphere going back in time. He also took into consideration recent data from American scientist Samuel Pierpont Langley regarding how much of the sun's energy the Earth's atmosphere allows in and how much it traps.

Arrhenius spent a year doing hand-written calculations to prove his hypothesis. When he completed his calculations in 1896, he concluded that if the amount of carbon dioxide in the atmosphere was cut in half versus its level present at his time, Europe's temperature would decrease by four to five degrees Celsius (seven to nine degrees Fahrenheit). He had created mankind's first climate model.

Arvid Högbom then set out to test whether Arrhenius' calculations concerning the relationship between the carbon dioxide level in the atmosphere and atmospheric temperatures applied to Earth's atmosphere in the real world. As part of his investigation, Högbom calculated the amount of carbon dioxide being released into the atmosphere by human's coal burning and industrial activities. Upon completion, he realized that the level of carbon dioxide in the atmosphere was slowly increasing because of mankind's activities.

Once Högbom completed his investigation and calculations, he and Arrhenius concluded that the addition of carbon dioxide to the Earth's atmosphere by mankind could cause the Earth's temperatures to warm over a long period of time. They predicted that such warming would occur over thousands of years. Arrhenius calculated if carbon dioxide doubled from the level it stood at the time of his investigation, the Earth's atmosphere would someday warm by five to six degree Celsius (nine to eleven degrees Fahrenheit).

The suggestion that the release of greenhouse gases by humans could warm the Earth's atmosphere remained a largely unaccepted scientific concept that few in the scientific community agreed with during the first half of the 20th century. This was because of a lack of confirmation that carbon dioxide high in the atmosphere was actually capable of blocking the escape of the Sun's infrared heat radiation and was ultimately responsible for heating the Earth's atmosphere.

Carbon dioxide's role in heating the planet wasn't accepted by the scientific community at large until the 1950s. At that time, scientists performed additional research into the matter using recently introduced computers that provided dramatically increased computational power to prove carbon dioxide's heating capability in the upper atmosphere. They also determined that oceans could absorb only a fraction of the carbon dioxide put into the atmosphere versus what the scientific community believed up to that point, which indicated carbon dioxide played a larger role in warming of the atmosphere than previously thought.

During the late 1950s and 1960s, a few scientists warned that the accumulation of greenhouse gases in the atmosphere could cause a problematic warming of the planet in the not too distant future. This was before a sustained global warming trend had been identified. At that time, the global average temperature was actually in a slight cooling trend due to cyclical influences from the world's oceans and the release of aerosols (tiny dust particles) into the atmosphere by mankind's expansive industrial activities, which reduced the amount of Sun radiation reaching the Earth's lower atmosphere and surface.

Before the connection between fossil fuel burning and a projected future increase in global temperature became a widely known problem and a political hot potato, scientists alerted petroleum and coal industry leaders, and the United States President Lyndon Johnson that burning carbon-based energy products would cause global warming in future decades.

In 1957, Edward Teller, the world-renowned Hungarian born American theoretical physicist who played a key role in the development of the hydrogen bomb made an address to the American Chemical Society. During the address he warned that burning carbon-based fuels was increasing the amount of carbon dioxide in the atmosphere, which would "act in the same way as a greenhouse and will raise the temperature at the surface" and eventually "an appreciable part of the polar ice might melt."

Teller also spoke at a symposium in New York City that was put together by the American Petroleum Institute and the Columbia Graduate School of Business in 1959 to celebrate the centennial of the American oil industry. At the symposium, he warned the attendees, many of whom were high-ranking persons within the oil industry, that the accumulation of carbon dioxide in the atmosphere would cause the natural greenhouse effect to be amplified to the point at which it "will be sufficient to melt the icecap and submerge New York. All the coastal cities would be covered, and since a considerable percentage of the human race lives in coastal regions, I think that this chemical contamination is more serious than most people tend to believe."

President Johnson was made aware of the potential for human induced warming of the atmosphere when the American Association for the Advancement of Science provided the President a report in 1965 titled, "Restoring the Quality of Our Environment." The report brought to Johnson's attention their scientific opinion that increases in carbon dioxide from humans burning fossil fuels would eventually cause the Earth's temperature to rise, which would lead to melting of the ice caps, sea level to rise, and the acidification of both fresh and sea water.

The coal industry was made aware the connection between burning coal and a predicted warming of the Earth's atmosphere in a 1966 issue of a coal industry publication called the Mining Congress Journal. In that issue, James R. Garvey, who was the president of Bituminous Coal Research Inc. warned his fellow coal industry leaders, "There is evidence that the amount of carbon dioxide in the Earth's atmosphere is increasing rapidly as a result of the combustion of fossil fuels. If the future rate of increase continues as it is at the present, it has been predicted that, because the carbon dioxide envelope reduces radiation, the temperature of the Earth's atmosphere will increase and that vast changes in the climates of the Earth will result. Such changes in temperature will cause melting of the polar icecaps, which, in turn, would result in the inundation of many coastal cities, including New York and London."

The American Petroleum Institute was provided a second warning in 1968 when they received a report on air pollution that they commissioned from the Stanford Research Institute. The report which was titled, "Sources, Abundance, and Fate of Gaseous Atmospheric Pollutants" warned the petroleum industry trade group of future global temperature increases and resulting impacts due to carbon dioxide releases into the atmosphere associated with burning petroleum and other fossil fuels.

Scott looked up the 1968 American Petroleum Institute report on the Internet and was astounded to read a passage that was a direct warning to the petroleum industry concerning the future danger associated with emission of carbon dioxide into the atmosphere, "... man is now engaged in a vast geophysical experiment with his environment, the Earth. Significant temperature changes are almost certain to occur by the year 2000 and these could bring about climate changes." Upon reading this, Scott felt angry and thought, "Amazing! Despite all their denials for decades, the oil companies have known all along about carbon dioxide's global warming connection!"

In 1975 the term "global warming" was coined when Columbia University Professor Wally Broecker published a paper called "Climate Change: Are We on the Brink of a Pronounced Global Warming?" in Science magazine. This was just before the sustained move upward in global temperatures started during the 1980s, continuing to the present day that Scott lived in, with some brief pauses along the way.

Learning all this, Scott had a clear understanding that high-ranking government and industry officials had knowledge of the global warming catastrophe that his generation faced, well before it was common knowledge among ordinary people. He knew they had put their own self-interests ahead of the common good, as they ignored the early warnings of a coming planetary climate crisis.

It seemed to Scott that not only did they fail to act in a responsible way, the coal and petroleum industries had made conscious decisions to cast doubt on the climate science that they knew to be true. They also funded efforts to smear climate scientists, lobbied governments to pull funding set aside for climate science research, and pressured governments to not pass laws that were proposed to address global warming. Their nefarious actions were carried out to ensure their products would remain in high demand, so they would continue to reap hefty profits.

Despite his growing understanding of the reality of global warming and mankind's role in causing it, Scott avoided conflicts with papa Joe about the topic by continuing to show interest in what his grandfather had to say while avoiding any contentious discussions. He understood that many in his grandfather's generation had been propagandized by public relations campaigns funded by the coal and petroleum industries. Such efforts included paying scientists and pundits to publish papers, write articles, participate on panels, and do presentations that raised questions about whether carbon dioxide from burning fossil fuels was responsible for the observed warming of the

Earth; offering many alternative explanations meant to muddy people's opinions.

Although he was acutely aware of the reality of the looming climate crisis, he felt it was useful to hear the other side's arguments no matter how fleeting they were becoming with each passing year, as the effects of global warming continued to manifest themselves in increasingly destructive ways throughout the world. He knew it was something his grandfather enjoyed talking about, so he just went along with it to humor him, knowing the world his generation was inheriting would face difficult climate problems that his grandfather's generation failed to address or in some respects even acknowledge.

Scott accepted that papa Joe and millions of others had made up their minds (with the assistance of well-funded propaganda efforts) and wouldn't do anything to solve the problem of global warming in the twilight of their lives. He understood that his grandfather's generation had dropped the ball and left the problem to future generations to solve. He knew it was going to be up to younger generations to step up and do something to head off the worst effects of global warming.

Chapter 4
A Rite of Passage

Since he was home-schooled, there was no graduation ceremony for Scott when he turned eighteen and was done with his schooling. Instead, his parents had a small party in their home to celebrate his accomplishments and transition into adulthood with friends and family.

As the party was winding down, papa Joe turned towards Scott with tears in his eyes and leaned unnaturally towards him. Scott's dad reflexively put his arms on papa Joe's shoulders to straighten him and his mom looked at them both with a great amount of concern.

Sobbing a bit as everyone looked at him in a perplexed manner, papa Joe said, "My tears are tears of both sadness and joy. Sadness that I know I am reaching the end of the line in my life, but great happiness that my grandson has turned into such a fine young man."

There was a sense of relief in the room, as papa Joe's family had been bracing for bad news. Scott hugged his grandfather and said, "Thanks so much for all you did to raise me and teach me about the great outdoors. It will have a lasting impression on me for the rest of my life. I will think of you every time I use one of the skills you taught me."

Papa Joe smiled a bit and replied, "It was my duty Scott." Everyone smiled. He then continued with a hesitant excitement in his voice, "I have been squirreling away money since you were born in case you had aspirations to go to college, but since you don't want to take that path, I want you to give you the money I have saved so you can see the world before you settle down. I wished I could have traveled the world as a young man, but here I am in my 80s and I don't see it ever happening, so I want you to realize my dreams."

Scott's mom gasped, while his dad smiled. They had no idea that papa Joe was going to give Scott such an incredible gift.

Scott was filled with joy. It was something he dreamed about doing ever since he started reading about the diverse world in which he lived. But he never thought he'd be able to fulfill his dreams given his modest existence. He lunged at papa Joe and gave him a big hug saying, "Thanks so much papa Joe, you're the best! This is something I've also always wanted to do." His grandfather smiled knowing that he had given his grandson a unique gift that would benefit him greatly over his lifetime.

Chapter 5
In Search of Global Warming

Scott planned his trip in a somewhat unusual way that he didn't let his parents or grandfather know about. Besides planning on seeing some famous places and wonders of the world, he planned to visit areas that were feeling the impacts of global warming to see how global warming was affecting the world in which he lived and what was being done to prepare for the uncertain future.

As he got ready for his trip, he felt as if he was living a dream. It seemed surreal as he surfed the Internet figuring out places to visit and made travel arrangements to visit them.

His first stop was the Canadian Rockies. It was more mountainous and picturesque than the part of Canada he lived in, but similar in some respects. What interested him were the glaciers in the Rockies that were receding as the Earth warmed.

He wanted to see evidence of glacial melting and retreat firsthand, so he went on a tour of the famous Athabasca Glacier in Jasper National Park that had receded more than two kilometers over the past 161 years. It was famous because of its accessibility being situated next to the Icefields Parkway and its well-documented retreat as Earth warmed. It was one of the most visible signs of global warming from the late 20th century into the middle 21st century.

After he departed the tour bus, he stood looking up at the glacier in the distance and markers that lay ahead of him. Each marker indicated the extent of the glacier at a point in time over the past 161 years. The oldest marker, which indicated the glaciers extent in 1890, was next to the Icefields Parkway.

It took him about forty minutes to walk up the alpine valley that once held the mighty glacier to reach the glacier's current terminus approximately two kilometers from the parking area along the Icefields Parkway. Once there, he stood looking up at what remained of the mammoth ice formation as it disappeared into the Columbia Icefield high up in the Rockies above. As he looked at the majestic glacier, he thought with some despair, "Someday over the next century this entire glacier will be gone. What will that mean for the rest of the world?"

As he turned around to walk back down to where his tour bus was by the Icefields Parkway his mood lightened up tremendously, his jaw dropped, and his breath was literally taken away as he looked out at the most spectacular view he'd ever been lucky enough to see. The Canadian Rockies in all their glory lay in front of him, from ice and snow-capped peaks to evergreen and boulder covered slopes to emerald lakes. It was a sight to behold and cherish. For a few moments, he forgot about everything going on in the world and stood mesmerized by the natural beauty that stood before him.

After his incredible trip to the Rockies, he took a train eastward across the Canadian prairies and past the scenic lakes and farms of Ontario, arriving in Toronto for the next leg of his trip.

Besides having some seasonal shifts, such as a longer, warmer, and wetter summer season and a milder yet still rather cold winter season, Toronto hadn't seen a lot of impacts from global warming yet. But, being a Canadian, it was a city Scott always wanted to visit, and it didn't disappoint him. It had a lot more excitement and action than he ever experienced during his visits to Whitehorse.

Next, he took a bus to Niagara Falls to see its wonderful natural beauty and power. He was in awe as he watched the deluge of water cascade over the falls with incredible force. Again, he had a few moments where nothing mattered except the raw beauty of nature that stood in front of him.

After seeing the falls, he made his way by train to New York City. As the train sped along the east bank of the Hudson River towards the Big Apple, he could see water lapping up against the railroad embankment in places. As he took in the beauty of the Hudson Valley, he wondered how much longer such train rides would be possible since the Hudson was a tidal river connected to the Atlantic Ocean and the water-level train line would eventually be overtaken by the rising tidal river.

New York was another city he always wanted to visit after reading so much about it over the years. It reminded him of Toronto, but it had a faster pace, which he found a bit overwhelming but enjoyed all the same.

Being directly on the Atlantic Ocean, New York City had felt the impacts of global warming in more visible ways than inland cities had to date. The historic Superstorm Sandy in 2012 was just the first of three superstorms/hurricanes to affect the New York City area by the time Scott arrived. Fueled by warmer ocean temperatures and jet stream patterns that had been altered by the changing climate, these monstrous storms did major damage to the city's infrastructure and caused significant harm to some of its inhabitants.

Superstorm Sandy served as an early wake-up call to political leaders that climate change can and will have significant negative impacts going forward. City leaders undertook measures to fortify the city's storm defenses, which helped the metropolis endure the two superstorms that followed. However, considerable damaged was still incurred, especially from wind that was in excess of anything ever experienced in the area and extensive flooding in low lying areas close to the ocean that had not yet been protected by the city's climate change mitigation program.

The days he spent in New York City were tranquil and sunny. He enjoyed seeing the city skyline from rooftop bars and the High Line trail. He also enjoyed exploring its various neighborhoods and sitting at cafes people-watching. He found the variety of people he saw walking by on a Manhattan sidewalk to be fascinating.

As he explored the extensive parks that ran along the waterfront areas, he saw many indications of a city that was preparing itself for rising sea level and future superstorms and hurricanes. Major climate mitigation construction projects were in full swing along the waterfronts he visited in Manhattan, Queens, and Brooklyn.

He read an interesting display put up by the city near a construction site that explained that raising of land and construction of flood walls were an effort to provide interim protection to low-lying areas that city planners had determined would otherwise go underwater in coming years due to rising sea level. The one thing that concerned Scott when he read the display was the fact that the flood walls were being constructed in anticipation of just a two meter (six-and-a-half-foot) rise in sea level in the future.

He thought, "That will not help if the worst-case scenario sea level rise occurs in the future. When mitigating risk, don't you build protections to the worst-case scenario threshold or at least to a reasonably high threshold?" Of course, he realized that the enormous cost associated with building maximized flood protection for a distant event that may not even happen was the reason worst-case protection would not be built.

He was fascinated by an ongoing debate in the local media about whether it would be cheaper to eventually abandon low-lying parts of New York City or to implement an expensive plan that included raising low-lying parts high enough to withstand 10 meters (33 feet) of sea level rise. This was high enough to withstand a moderate sea level rise, but certainly not high enough to hold back the ocean if a worst-case scenario played out in the long run and sea level rose 60 meters (197 feet) or more.

When he was done visiting New York, he took a train to Miami. He could have flown to the warm southern Florida city, but he preferred ground travel to see as much of the landscape of the countries he was visiting as possible. He also liked the fact that train travel left a smaller carbon footprint than air travel, since trains emit one-third to two-thirds less carbon dioxide per passenger than planes.

He found Miami to be a beautiful part of the world to visit, but also a part that was already experiencing major impacts from rising sea level caused by global warming. The old "sunny day King Tide flooding" problem that had emerged forty years ago had morphed into regular high tide flooding for the lowest lying neighborhoods in and around the city.

Unlike New York City, which had an air of optimism that the city would adapt to climate change and rising sea level, leaders in the Miami area were facing stark choices driven by the rising ocean.

The City of Miami Beach had given up efforts to save its South Beach neighborhood, and it had been abandoned. There was a time in the early 21st century when city planners were optimistic that measures could be taken to keep the ocean's waters out of South Beach, but those times had passed quickly as sea level rise accelerated beyond their ability to take action to protect the lowest neighborhood in their city. Now the battleground against the constantly rising sea was focused on higher parts of the Miami area.

On a visit to the University of Miami's Sea Level Rise Impact Learning Center, he read about extensive planning that was in progress to build sea walls to protect what was left of Miami at an incredible cost. However, that was not the only point of view on display. There was a section that highlighted the views of scientists that questioned whether it was even worth trying to save the greater Miami area from seawater inundation. They argued that if the worst-case scenario played out, the ocean would swamp the entire Miami area and much of low-lying Florida with seawater despite construction of the proposed modest sea walls.

Scientists featured in this section questioned whether the whole Miami area and other low-lying parts of Florida should just be given back to the Atlantic Ocean by implementing a plan to retreat to higher ground instead of spending hundreds of billions of dollars to save the city and surrounding area from an optimistically low anticipated sea level rise. The efforts to protect the area, in their view, would someday prove futile as global warming kicked into high gear and the ocean topped the sea walls.

Such drastic recommendations were simply ignored by city leaders. Who wanted to be the politician that told everyone to pack up, abandon their properties as worthless, and move to parts unknown, for something scientists were predicting might occur hundreds of years in the future?

The tremendous cost of protecting the Miami area from the rising ocean reminded Scott of past politicians' arguments that he had read regarding their ardent position that taking actions to prevent global warming by eliminating fossil fuel use would be too costly to implement. He mused, "We could have spent some money and effort years ago to keep a lid on global warming, but now we're debating whether to pay a lot more to deal with its consequences, and what is being proposed may not even be enough."

While he found it enjoyable to be hanging out on the local beaches and outdoor restaurants soaking in the South Florida sunshine, the realization that the entire area could be underwater in just a few generations put Scott in a melancholy mood. It was especially odd for him to feel sad given how happy so many people around him were as they enjoyed the warm sunny Miami weather. He hoped the next leg of his trip, which included some great historic sites in Europe, would elevate his mood.

Scott landed in Amsterdam, Holland. A trip around the world that focused on global warming impacts had to include a visit to the country that had been fighting off the sea for centuries, well before global warming and rising sea level had become a mainstream concern.

While the Dutch had been incredibly innovative and resourceful at keeping the sea off of the land on which they lived, Scott was profoundly saddened to learn that even the hearty Dutch who had masterminded flood control were making plans to abandon the lowest-lying parts of their country, if moderate sea level rise occurred in the future. This knowledge reinforced in his mind the reality that the forces of nature can be stronger than mankind's will and intellect. He thought, "We can't just address the symptoms of this problem. We have to work with nature to restore balance to the climate and find technological fixes that eliminate the causes of global warming, not just deal with the symptoms."

He headed to Greta Thunberg's home city of Stockholm, Sweden to visit a learning center that had been set up to honor their local hero and current Prime Minister, who as a teenager challenged the world in 2019 to take on the climate crisis and implement solutions. He found the vibe in Stockholm to be much more positive than Florida or Holland had been.

The learning center was dedicated to solutions to the climate crisis, including ending the use of fossil fuels entirely with viable plans to switch to 100% renewable energy and planting trees on an unprecedented scale. It also included explanations regarding promising carbon removal technologies that had been proposed and were being researched. Seeing this and talking to the friendly locals who were happy that their city had become the focal point for solutions to the climate crisis gave Scott a renewed sense of hope and optimism.

He then went on to visit London, Paris, Madrid, the Swiss Alps, and major cities in Germany. This part of his trip was a time when he truly felt at ease. While he took the time to discover global warming impacts in each area he visited, he also enjoyed learning about local history, taking in the beautiful sights of Europe, sitting at cafes, and talking to the locals whenever he could. He was feeling upbeat and was excited to see more.

He hopped on a train to Venice, Italy. This was another must-see city on his tour of global warming impacts. He timed his trip so the city's squares and alleyways would be free of water. With the sea level rise that had already occurred, Venice was flooded on many days of the year during times of seasonally high tides and storms.

He found Venice to be on the quiet side compared to other European cities. Many of the people and shop owners had already abandoned the city where canals served as thoroughfares rather than streets, in anticipation of the inevitable permanent flooding that would occur in the future.

Given its proximity to the Adriatic Sea and since waterways snaked through the city, there was no viable engineering solution that could keep Venice from being taken back by the sea. A flood barrier that was proposed during the early part of the 21st century had been abandoned as too impractical and expensive.

He felt lucky to have a chance to see the world-renowned unique city, as many others before him had, before it was completely abandoned and captured by the sea.

He then made his way to Florence and through the picturesque Tuscany and Umbria countryside, winding up in Rome. Not much had changed in these parts of Italy. The air temperature was hot, but that was not unusual for Italy during the summer. What was unusual was the extreme periods of heat and the longer summer season overall versus times past.

Rome was being impacted by the climate crisis differently than many other European cities. The global temperature rise that had occurred to date and subsequent major famines in Africa had caused a sizable migration of climate refugees into Rome, which was stressing the city's resources.

Scott realized that mass migrations of climate refugees would accelerate in many parts of the world as the impacts of global warming became worse over time and made areas close to the equator unlivable because of extreme heat and drought. He understood that it wouldn't just be Africa that would have climate refugees looking for somewhere to live. People from low-lying parts of Florida and Holland, and any area near sea level, would someday find themselves refugees of the climate crisis.

Scott walked through the ruins of the Roman Empire, which was an incredible outdoor museum in the center of Rome that offered a peek into the ancient past of human civilization. As he walked past the ruins, he couldn't help thinking about what it must have been like to be alive during the great Roman Empire that existed 2,000 years ago. He thought, "The Romans couldn't have even imagined how the seemingly unmovable forces of nature could be set into motion in such a way to threaten the very existence of mankind."

Upon finishing his European tour in Rome, his next stops were low-lying parts of Asia that were feeling the effects of rising sea level and rising temperatures. Scott first visited Shanghai, China, a city that was expecting a considerable amount of sea level rise impacts due to its proximity to the Pacific Ocean and its huge population that lived within a few feet of sea level. Even the mighty Chinese government could not figure out a way to hold back the ocean forever and was making plans to relocate hundreds of millions of residents from low-lying parts of China to higher elevations. Not an easy task for a country with nearly two billion people and a shortage of land.

In response to the climate crisis and the population pressures the country was facing, China re-instituted the controversial "one child policy" to prevent the population from increasing. This time, China added another layer to the controversial policy that included a "citizen score" and "intelligence score" as part of the official authorization to have a child.

Chinese authorities used complex methods of capturing data and scoring citizen compliance with government policies and directives. They also created a personal intelligence test to assess citizens' intelligence and used the findings to assign each citizen an intelligence score. Only those who scored highly in these two categories received official government approval to have a child. The Chinese not only wanted to stop population growth, they also wanted to engineer a compliant and intelligent citizenry.

Upon learning of the latest move by the Chinese government into totalitarian control of its citizens' lives, Scott found himself shaking as he thought, "Wow! That's brutal!" He knew an ever-expanding population was contributing to the worsening climate crisis, but as someone who came from a country that valued individual freedom, it was quite shocking to hear how intrusive the Chinese government was in its citizens' affairs. As he later learned through reading, several other countries with authoritarian governments were considering instituting similar policies because of growing concerns about population expansion and its effect on the environment.

After a rather brief visit to China, Scott made his way through the beautiful tropical beach areas of Asia from Thailand to Indonesia. While it was easy to forget about global warming as he spent time on beaches in a tropical paradise, he was reminded that life was becoming increasingly difficult for the island's inhabitants. Due to global warming's impacts on the oceans, which made them warmer and more acidic, fish stocks and catches were diminishing. This was making it hard for humans that relied upon seafood for subsistence to remain on the islands. Some low-lying areas of the islands were being abandoned because of rising sea level. In addition, typhoons were more frequent and powerful than ever, affecting the islands in terrible ways.

Scott enjoyed traveling through the islands but felt a bit of the odd melancholy that he had felt in Miami, knowing such beautiful places were slowly dying because of a planet that was reacting to two centuries of pollutants being dumped into its atmosphere. Paradise was sadly fading on many beautiful tropical islands.

On his way to Australia, Scott read a very disturbing article about the race by various nations and oil companies to explore for oil in the thawing Arctic polar regions. Global warming and the subsequent melting of ice sheets had freed up areas in the far reaches of the Arctic to oil exploration and it turned out that there was a lot of oil to be had in the far north. With the Arctic Ocean ice-free for half of the year and nearby land areas losing ice cover, the once inhospitable top of the world was quickly becoming a free-for-all of oil exploration.

With some notable exceptions, many countries were committed to reducing carbon emissions and had done so in their power generation and industrial sectors. But the world economy still primarily ran on oil, especially for transportation. It didn't help that oil prices had been climbing for years due to slackening production from aging oil fields. With pressure increasing from the masses of people that wanted cheap energy, politicians in many countries brushed aside concerns about global warming and approved applications for exploration of potential oil deposits in the formerly frozen Arctic region. It was a very disturbing development for those like Scott who were growing increasingly concerned about the long-term effects of dumping carbon dioxide into the atmosphere.

Scott had a sinking feeling in his stomach as he read about this race to produce oil in the Arctic. He knew it was bad news as far as keeping carbon dioxide emissions in check and would make the global warming situation much worse over time. It was at that moment, as he flew in a jetliner over the Pacific Ocean that was burning petroleum-derived jet fuel and spewing carbon dioxide into the atmosphere that he decided he would seek a career that would help move mankind off of fossil fuels. He knew it was imperative that the senseless drilling for oil in the Arctic had to stop and he was ready to do his part to help mankind kick its fossil fuels addiction. It was a seminal moment in his life that literally set him on his life's career passion. He was excited about his epiphany, even though he wasn't sure how it was going to work out.

Scott was both worried and excited by the time he got to Australia. He was concerned about the environmental impacts he had seen but was amazed at how different and varied the world was compared to where he grew up in northern Canada and was excited to see more.

He started off spending a few days in Sydney where he came across the Australia Climate Change Education Center. Like many other coastal cities, Sydney was busy preparing for a future with higher sea level. What he really found interesting at the education center was their exhibit on the great wildfires of the late 2010s and 2020s. The enormous out of control wildfires shaped Australia's future like no other climate event.

Despair over the massive damage caused by the fires and worries that cities such as Sydney would run out of water due to the increasingly hot climate led to a sea-change in attitudes among Australians. The country collectively decided that it had to be a net positive influence in the growing movement to address the climate crisis. It led to the passing of laws to phase out the use and export of fossil fuels, to secure water supplies using desalination and purification technologies, to address rising sea level, and to make efforts to restore the Great Barrier Reef. It gave Scott a good feeling knowing he was standing in a country that took climate change seriously and was addressing the problems associated with it.

After a few days in Sydney, he set off for Queensland to see the famed Great Barrier Reef off the northeast coast of

Australia. The decline of the reef had long been held out as a "canary in the coal mine" by environmentalists trying to warn people of future dangers associated with global warming. Much of the Great Barrier Reef was under duress and had turned white, a process called bleaching. This was because of warmer ocean temperatures causing coral to expel a white alga, leaving the reef to look like a white corpse. The reef was not technically dead when it turned white but was rather sick and more prone to dying. By the time Scott arrived, large swaths of the world-renowned reef had turned white and were in danger of dying.

Scott was happy to learn that all was not lost. Scientists in Australia found innovative ways to help the Great Barrier Reef regenerate its coral despite the ocean's inhospitable temperature. It involved creating coral in a laboratory capable of surviving at higher temperatures than they normally would, then transplanting them onto the Great Barrier Reef. They also used an unusual method of bringing the fish back to the reef. They mimicked the sounds associated with a healthy underwater reef to lure fish back to the reef. Once the coral had taken hold in its underwater environment and fish had returned, the sound machines were removed, and the reef was restored.

Scott took a boat trip to see a small portion of the rehabilitated reef firsthand. It was quite a sight to behold, not just witnessing the reef's natural beauty firsthand, but also discovering the best aspects of human spirit and intellect being used to save an underwater treasure. He was hopeful that such efforts would someday restore the entire Great Barrier Reef to its former glory.

Australians had also become a leader in figuring out ways to run their society on 100% renewable energy to meet all the country's electricity needs. Being a geographically isolated country with an environmentally conscious population allowed Australia to innovate and become energy self-sufficient in ways which made them the envy of other countries. Of course, this was no easy task since more than half the cars on the road ran on electricity, which created considerable demand for electricity. They used their vast wind and sun resources, as well as wave and tidal sources of renewable energy, along with utility-scale battery storage to achieve the 100% renewable electricity threshold.

He concluded his visit down under with a trip to the spectacular Uluru (Ayers Rock) in the center of the country. Scott stood in awe as the sun set on the iconic rock formation that towered above the dry and sparsely vegetated Outback landscape. As he sat and ate a snack by the picturesque rock, he was treated with a passing mob of red kangaroos, which locals told him was quite rare.

He spent the night in Alice Springs, which was the closest hub of civilization to Uluru, making a point of staying at a world-famous eco-lodge that was known for its use of innovative environmentally friendly technologies. The lodge included rooms that were geothermally cooled by the ground just a few meters under the surface and electricity that was delivered by solar roof tiles with battery backup, so power was available day and night rain or shine.

He went for a late meal in the lodge's bar and was greeted by the friendliest bartender he had ever met. Australians had a reputation for being friendly and Scott understood why. "Good evening mate. Hope you're enjoying your trip to our corner of the world. What'll it be?" the bartender asked with a warm friendly tone.

Scott replied, "Oh, ahh good evening. I think I'm in the mood for a cold cider right about now. Took a trip to Uluru today and I'm totally parched."

The bartender soon returned with a frosty mug that contained ice and hard cider and said, "Here you are. So, you visited our friend Uluru. Hope she treated you right. My name's Noah by the way."

"Thanks!" Scott replied and took a big swig of cider. "I'm Scott. Yeah, it was a quite a thrill seeing the sun set on that big old rock. Who would have thought a rock could that beautiful?"

Noah smiled and said, "Oh, they come from all over the world to see old Uluru. You'd think we locals would get sick of seeing it, but it's one of those wonders of nature that you never tire of laying your eyes on."

"So far from home, are you a Yankee or South African? I can't quite make out your accent," Noah asked inquisitively.

Scott smiled a bit and replied, "Can't make out my accent, eh?"

"Oh, you're a Canuck! Well, welcome to the warm country!" Noah responded cheerfully.

"Yeah, I'm actually from a remote part of northern Canada called the Yukon. My accent differs from most Canadians; probably due to how isolated we are from the rest of Canada. You aren't the first one to have trouble figuring out where I'm from," Scott responded as he downed some more cider.

Noah replied, "I see mate. So, is the world melting up there? Because we've been suffering an awful heat down under here for years, I'll tell ya."

Scott, happy to talk to someone interested in global warming replied, "It's not like it's melting all over, but there are signs of warming like permafrost melting, ground heaving, and glaciers receding. I've been traveling the world the past few months to witness signs of global warming. There's no doubt, it's happening and it's starting to impact some places in obvious ways." He finished his cider and ordered another one with a cup of ice on the side, so he could make it last longer.

Noah placed a fresh pint of cider along with a cup of ice in front of Scott and said with a slight smile, "See that cup of ice."

"Yeah", Scott responded.

"Where do you think it came from?" Noah asked with a wry smirk.

Scott, feeling the effects of the first cider was amused at such an odd question and responded with an expression of doubt, "I dunno, a well, the sky, Antarctica?"

Noah bellowed with laughter, "Would you believe, the thin air?"

Scott replied with a bit of hesitation since he felt like he was being set up, "I'd have a hard time believing that."

Regaining his composure Noah said, "Us Aussies are a resourceful lot, especially here in the Outback. It's a desert. People shouldn't be living in a desert since it doesn't have much water. Given the warming we've experienced and population growth, many of us wouldn't be living here for lack of water. So, some smart bloke figured out a way to wring water out of the air and then purify it, so we can safely consume it. So, you're looking at ice that came from water that was wrung out of the thin Outback air. Pretty cool, right?"

"Yeah, that is cool, never heard of such a thing. How does it work?" Scott asked.

"Well, it's really not that complicated. I'm sure you've seen an air conditioner running?" Noah asked.

Scott responded, "Not until I took this trip. There are no air conditions in the Yukon, at least not yet."

Noah continued, "Okay then. Well when they run, they literally condense the air and remove moisture as part of their cooling process. This Aussie bloke figured out a way to enhance the process to run it 24/7 on renewable energy, then added a filtering system, and voila, you have drinkable water anywhere you need it. Even in the dry Outback desert there's plenty of moisture that this machine can wring out of the air."

Scott plunked a few ice cubes into his half-full pint and watched them melt as the bartender turned his attention to another customer. This revelation that drinkable water could be made out of thin air made him think about all the technological solutions various people had proposed to address global warming. After thinking it over for a while, he concluded, "Perhaps it's not so dire after all. Maybe we can figure out a technological fix to the climate crisis. We've got plenty of time to figure this all out."

He ate dinner and spent the evening chatting at the bar with other travelers from all over the world who found their way to Alice Springs. The next morning, he started a train journey through the Outback to where he started his Australian adventure, Sydney.

After traveling for three months, it was time to make his way home. He bid Australia a hearty goodbye as the plane turned to show Sydney Harbor in all its glory below.

On his flight from Sydney to Los Angeles, Scott was feeling optimistic about the future. He spent a good part of the long flight reading about various geoengineering solutions that had been proposed to reverse global warming. Some he felt were pie-in-the-sky and would never happen, but others seemed practical enough that they would likely work.

Los Angeles was another city that brought optimism to Scott's outlook. The city had lived in a climate crisis for its entire existence; being built in an arid part of North America where human occupation on any large scale was always a challenge due to its dry climate and lack of potable water. Yet, the city's resolve ensured its citizens had the water they needed to survive and prosper. The Los Angeles area had also been successfully dealing with serious air pollution problems since the middle of the 20th century. The quest for a clean and livable environment made Los Angeles one of the most innovative and proactive cities in the world for eliminating air pollution associated with burning fossil fuels.

After spending a few days seeing the sites in Los Angeles, he made his way up the west coast of North

America on the West Coast Maglev, which extended from San Diego to Vancouver, British Columbia. The magnetically propelled train traveled at speeds approaching 500 miles per hour, making the trip from Los Angeles to San Francisco in just two hours. As he watched the State of California pass in a blur, he wondered what it was like taking this trip on an old steel wheel train before the Maglev was built.

On his way home he made stops in San Francisco, Portland, Seattle, and Vancouver. The story was the same in every city. While they were all beautiful and picturesque, there was an underlying foreboding about the future and what the warming climate would bring to their cities.

In most low-lying areas within the cities, the initial fortifications against sea level rise had been made. Like other parts of the world, debates were ongoing in each city about whether low-lying areas that would be inundated by significant sea level rise should be protected at a great cost or should just be abandoned and left to the sea. There were legitimate concerns raised about costs and whether the engineering controls would be effective or would eventually fail if the sea kept rising more than it was currently projected to rise.

On the bus back to Whitehorse, where his mom and grandfather were meeting him to take him home, Scott thought about all the sights he had seen while traveling around the world and the global warming impacts that he witnessed. The debates regarding what to do about low-lying areas subject to future sea level rises stuck in his mind. He thought, "What it really comes down to is that we do not know where this global warming will lead and how bad the impacts will ultimately be. We are literally gambling with our future by continuing practices that are contributing to the warming of our planet. Especially since we know that the response from Earth to all the global warming gases we've pumped into the atmosphere is not immediate and will take centuries to be fully realized."

As he collected his thoughts about what he had witnessed during his travels, Scott knew that he needed to take an active role in solutions to the looming climate crisis. He had made that decision on his way to Australia and intended to follow through with it.

As he walked off the bus at the Whitehorse bus station, he felt relieved to see two familiar faces, his mom and papa Joe. It was an awesome and memorable trip, but it was nice to see his family again. His mom gave him a big hug while papa Joe said, "Welcome back Scott!" Scott hugged his grandfather and thanked him for making the trip possible.

After settling into the SUV for the long drive back home, papa Joe asked, "So how'd it go? We received your e-postcards, but I'm sure they didn't tell the whole story."

Scott replied with a weary voice, "I'll tell you papa, the world is more beautiful and diverse than one can ever imagine. Seeing some of the sights I observed literally took my breath away. It was an indescribable feeling."

Papa Joe was pleased and smiled. Scott continued, "I can never thank you enough for the gift you gave me that allowed me to see our incredible planet. I'll have to tell you more later as I'm feeling pretty wiped out."

Papa Joe understood. Being an outdoorsman, he had spent weeks in the wilderness, and when he returned to his family, it took him a few days to get back to his usual self.

Scott stared out of the window at the rolling big-sky Yukon landscape as he thought about all he had witnessed over the past three months. After about twenty minutes, his mom broke the silence and asked him, "What do you feel like having for dinner? I can make you one of those barbecue pizzas that you love."

Scott didn't answer. He was fast asleep. She smiled at him and then back at papa Joe, who nodded at her.

Chapter 6
Moving On

As he reflected on what he had experienced during his trip, Scott had a broader understanding of the world and the real-world impacts global warming was having on the planet. He felt as though he had a real purpose in life as he was ready to join the movement to address what many called climate change. He liked to refer to it as global warming or simply as the climate crisis. After all, the problem was the warming and the crisis it was causing in the global climate. While he was growing up, he imagined himself scraping out a living working in the rugged Yukon like his ancestors had, but now he was driven by a strong desire to play a role in solving the global warming problem before it spun out of control.

Since his return from his globe-trekking journey, life was good. After spending a few months in the Yukon with his family, he moved to the City of Calgary in the Canadian province of Alberta. The province was known as Canada's oil country, since it contained tar sands oil deposits that had been mined for decades and turned into crude oil that was sold on the world oil market. At one time, tar sands mining and refining had been the engine of the region's economic growth. However, it had been on the decline for years due to environmental pressures and decreasing demand for oil products to run automobiles and trucks and to heat homes.

As the year turned to 2052, Scott found work as a solar power system installer in the Calgary area with an international solar company called WorldWide Solar, realizing his dream of working in an industry that was helping to reduce the impacts of global warming. He was brought on under an apprenticeship program that the company had put in place to train new solar installers.

By 2052, renewable energy had made considerable advancements in cost and efficiency. About a half of the automobiles and trucks in use around the world were running on electricity, much of which was derived from renewable energy. Yet, mankind was still using fossil fuels and was pouring carbon dioxide and other greenhouse gases into the atmosphere in amounts that were contributing to the heating of the planet. This was in part driven by the ever-expanding global population that now included over 10 billion people.

The 2016 Paris Climate Agreement had, for a time, resulted in a drop of carbon dioxide releases to target levels in many countries. However, the agreement ultimately proved ineffective as releases started increasing over time in many parts of the world. Political and population pressures led to weakening of carbon-reduction regulations and to clear cutting of forests in many countries, which led to an increase in the carbon dioxide level in the atmosphere. Some notable countries, such as China, the United States, and India, never met their Paris Climate Agreement emissions targets and were contributing greatly to carbon dioxide emissions in 2052.

As the Earth's atmosphere and oceans warmed in response to the rising carbon dioxide level, methane (CH_4) and carbon dioxide that had been frozen for millions of years in ice sheets, tundra, and beneath the ocean floors was released into the atmosphere at an increasing rate.

Frozen methane is a compound called methane hydrate that is comprised of methane gas molecules trapped inside frozen water crystals. Over time, as the atmosphere and oceans slowly warmed, methane hydrate melted and was liberated from its frozen state which released the methane gas it contained. The methane rose into the atmosphere and acted as a strong greenhouse gas in the upper atmosphere that accelerated the ongoing global temperature rise. Although frozen carbon dioxide releases were concerning, methane gas releases from frozen methane hydrate were particularly concerning to scientists and policy makers since methane is a potent global warming gas that is twenty-eight times more effective at warming the atmosphere than carbon dioxide over long periods of time.

Chapter 7
Collective Destruction

One evening while hanging out at his favorite watering hole, Scott got into a friendly discussion about global warming over a game of pool he was playing with an acquaintance named Jake who worked for what remained of the Alberta oil industry.

After Jake sank the three and five balls, then missed on the seven, he turned to Scott and made a typical skeptical statement, "You know that the recent global warming has been caused by the Sun. The Sun is the reason the Earth is warm enough to support life and is enormous. It must have a bigger influence on Earth's climate than greenhouse gases we are spewing."

Scott sunk the ten, twelve, and fifteen balls, then missed his next shot. As the cue ball came to a stop, he replied, "At times in the past that has been true; the Sun's increasing intensity has been the primary driver of Earth's temperature. However, the Sun cannot be responsible for the warming we've experienced since the 1980s, because the Sun has been in a weakening trend since then and has been sending less of its radiation towards Earth. This is due to a natural cycle that the Sun goes through over decades and centuries. It is currently in the cooling part of the cycle." He then pulled up a graph on his phone that showed decreasing Sun radiation plotted against the increasing global temperature trend.

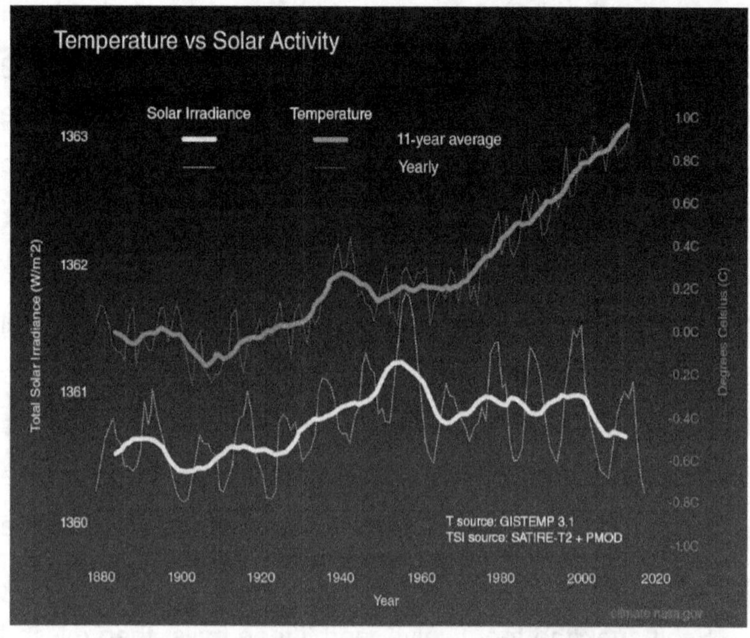

Figure 1. Sun Radiance Versus Average Global Temperature

Source: climate.nasa.gov

Jake shrugged in agreement as there was no doubt after looking at the graph that the Sun had not been driving the recent warming of the Earth, because it had indeed been weakening.

They broke to get some beer, and the friendly discussion continued at the bar. Jake said, "Our releases of greenhouse gases cannot be causing global warming because we cannot possibly affect something as vast and versatile as the Earth's atmosphere and climate. It is arrogant of us to believe that we can have a significant impact on something as large as the entire planet's atmosphere and climate." To a skeptic like Jake, such notions were rooted in mankind's hubris and a sense of importance that were not in line with reality in his opinion.

Scott knew that even though many scientific studies and published papers had used an enormous volume of scientifically gathered data to make the connection between mankind's carbon dioxide releases and global warming, they were of no use when discussing this topic with someone who was a global warming skeptic. Jake was one of many who had essentially been convinced to not trust scientists, so citing scientists' conclusions about mankind's responsibility for warming the planet was useless. To counter such a mindset, Scott had thought of a great analogy that any outdoorsman or sensible person would understand.

As they returned to their game of pool, Scott asked, "Have you seen an ant and thought how insignificant the littler critter is?"

Jake replied, "Sure have, but what's that got to do with anything?"

Scott replied, "Have you ever seen a tree that was totally destroyed by carpenter ants or termites or one of those nature programs that shows an entire segment of forest decimated by colonies of ants run amok?"

Jake took a shot at the 6 ball that missed the mark by a few millimeters. He then replied with a bit of suspicion, as he knew Scott was onto something but didn't know what it was, "Well sure. It's incredible what those little buggers can do to a big tree or an entire area of forest when they're all working together. I've seen it myself several times. What's your point?"

Scott sunk the 9 ball, then shot the 8 ball in the side pocket to win the game and replied, "Well, if millions of little carpenter ants or termites can easily destroy something enormously bigger than they are such as a large tree or an area of forest, what makes you think us little old humans cannot have the same effect on something enormously bigger than ourselves such as our atmosphere? One ant on its own cannot damage anything that's much bigger than itself, and the same could be said of one human. But when they are all working together, numerous ants can cause massive destruction. The same principle can be applied to humans. With billions of humans on Earth and our numbers increasing daily, our collective actions can have real impacts on a much larger thing than ourselves, like our atmosphere and climate system."

Jake had a look like he was considering what Scott had just said then grudgingly nodded in agreement and said, "I see your point. I never thought of it that way. We're just like those little buggers the way they collectively destroy things. Termites nearly destroyed an outbuilding on my property last summer until I discovered them and got rid of them."

Scott did not gloat about winning his friendly discussion with Jake. Instead he said, "You know Jake. I've spoken to a few people over the years that were either skeptical or outright deniers of man's role in causing global warming. I'll tell you what. In all honesty, I wish I was wrong, and the skeptics and deniers were right. I wish I was 100% wrong and could go home at the end of the evening knowing I was proven wrong. I certainly don't want global warming to spin out of control. I want the skeptics and deniers to be right and have the Earth's temperatures naturally return to a time when they were relatively stable, and we had no worries about the future of our climate. But, the data and science keep coming in and they are unfortunately telling us that it is the skeptics and deniers that are wrong and that we better prepare for a much warmer world and all the consequences that go along with it."

Jake was dumbfounded and after thinking it through smiled. He was never actually a hardcore skeptic or denier about the matter. He was just a product of his upbringing and the culture in which he lived and worked in, much as Scott's views as a child were a product of his upbringing in his early years. He thanked Scott and said he looked forward to meeting up with him again for another game of pool and interesting discussion.

Chapter 8
And Just Like That

After a long week of work, Scott did his regular Friday night thing, hanging at his favorite local bar, playing pool, and chatting with some friends he had made in Calgary. At the end of the evening, he walked back to his apartment and was so tired that he passed out on his bed with his clothes still on.

Shortly before he woke up, he had the strangest dream about places he had visited in different parts of the world just a year ago. Everywhere in his dream he saw lots of murky water closing in on beautiful memories from his travels. This lasted for what seemed like forever until he woke up in a hot sweat to the sound of a local community radio station that he had his alarm clock set to.

"Damn," he thought, "I must have accidentally set my alarm last night," as he rolled around on his bed in a groggy and disturbed mood. It was Saturday; there was no need to get up for work or for anything. He was so tired and wiped out that he couldn't pick himself up out of bed to turn off the radio, so he lay there with his clothes on from the prior night trying to process the strangely disturbing dream he had just before he had suddenly been woken up. After a few minutes, as he slowly woke up more, he started focusing on the radio broadcast.

He realized that the host was interviewing a local university Professor named Emanuel Goodspeed, Ph.D., a well-known expert regarding the effects of global warming throughout the world. The host asked, "So, in your estimation with the abrupt collapse of the Thwaites Glacier and connected parts of the West Antarctic ice sheet that started overnight we can expect a sea level rise of at least three meters throughout the world?" Scott was taken aback by what he heard and felt a sinking feeling in his stomach. He thought with despair, "This isn't supposed to be happening so soon."

Professor Goodspeed responded in a measured and authoritative tone, "Unfortunately, yes. If we can trust our calculations, then any areas exposed to the world's oceans will experience at least a three-meter rise once the collapse is complete over the next several weeks. In some areas the rise will be even greater due to local influences. The potential for this ice sheet to collapse is one thing scientists have worried about since global temperatures rose past the two-degree Celsius threshold a decade ago, and now it is actually happening a lot sooner than many thought it would."

As Scott lay in his bed stunned, he realized he must have been hearing this terrible news from the radio shortly before he woke up and it had affected his dream, filling it with murky water. His thought was interrupted by the host who asked with a bit of hesitation, "What uh then, <pause> does this mean for all the people who live within three meters of the oceans, such as low-lying parts of South Florida, Venice in Italy, or densely populated coastal cities in Asia?"

Professor Goodspeed quickly replied with the cold seriousness and calmness only a scientist could have in the face of such a calamity, "It means at least 500 million people around the world will be displaced from their homes over the next few days. It means many businesses will be incapable of operating and entire transit systems, tunnels, and low-lying roadways will be permanently flooded. It means the world will lose tens of millions of acres of low-lying farmable land. It means economic growth is going to be severely impacted as the economic centers of the world reel from flooding and trade grinds to a halt in many places. Unfortunately, what we are facing is the rapidly rising sea-level disaster that scientists have warned about for decades and it will impact mankind in very negative ways. For many, it means the end of life as they previously knew it. For some, it means they will lose their lives."

Professor Goodspeed paused, cleared his throat, then continued, "It also serves as another warning for those who live away from oceans, as we do in Alberta, that climate change is very real and will be very destructive over time in many ways that will also affect us. What concerns me, and I'm sure many of my colleagues, is that this ice sheet collapse occurred many years before it was predicted to occur by a consensus of researchers. This provides us an indication that the planet is warming, and the climate is changing faster than we expected in ways we don't fully understand. This is a troubling development."

Scott thought, "Wow!" and trembled with the realization of how devastating the news he just heard was. The host simultaneously said in an astonished voice "Wow!" echoing Scott's thoughts.

Scott turned off the radio and lay in his bed for another hour with a nauseous feeling in his stomach as he thought about all the places he had visited and the people he had met during his travels that were facing an imminent flooding disaster and how much the world was about to change. He felt comforted because he lived in Calgary, which is a land-locked city more than one thousand meters above sea-level but felt sad for the chaos that was about to unfold in highly populated areas across the world close to sea-level.

Considering the dramatic new developments, Scott could do little himself other than continue to work on installing solar power systems. He was already producing a very inconsequential carbon footprint. He drove an electric car that was powered by renewable solar and wind electricity that he purchased from a third-party electricity supplier. He purposely chose to live in a modern building that was heated and cooled using a non-polluting geothermal heating and cooling system, with the electricity it needed coming from renewable sources. He also adopted a vegan diet to avoid consuming meat and contributing to global warming through his diet.

Scott was amazed how diametrically different his views about global warming and lifestyle choices were compared to his grandfather who thought global warming was a bunch of made up nonsense that nobody should concern themselves with and certainly didn't warrant any lifestyle changes. He realized that it was not a generational gap; it was more like a generational canyon.

Instead of burying his head in the sand, Scott was eager to learn more about global warming. A few weeks after the unexpected sea level rise, he attended a lecture held by Professor Goodspeed at a local university that delved into the science of what was causing the planet to warm.

Professor Goodspeed explained, "Carbon is in all living things on our planet, including all of you. Earth has what is known as the carbon cycle which refers to the continuous and cyclical movement of carbon through the water, land, atmosphere, and just about any matter on Earth, including fossil fuels. When carbon was abundant in the atmosphere as carbon dioxide gas, Earth was warm. When it was frozen as a solid on the Earth's surface in glaciers and ice sheets and less abundant in the atmosphere, Earth was cool."

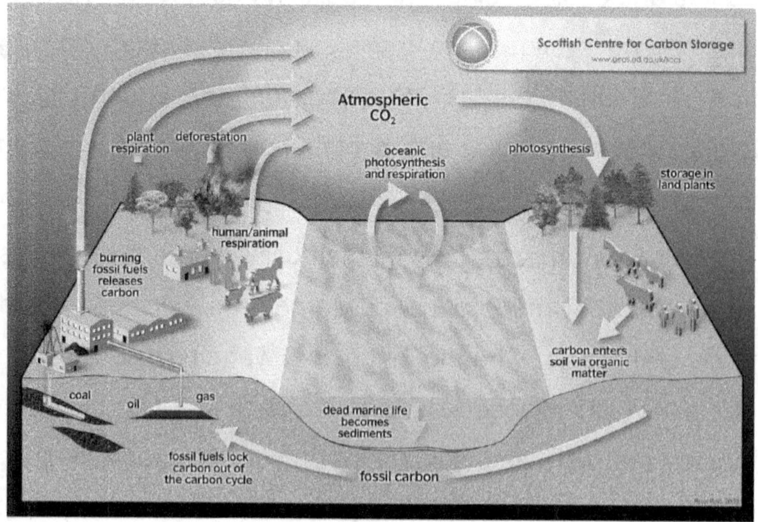

Figure 2. The Carbon Cycle

Source: Scottish Centre for Carbon Storage via commons.wikimedia.org

He continued, "Since the industrial revolution took hold during the 19th century, our burning of fossil fuels has transformed massive amounts of carbon from its liquid and solid states in which it has existed for millions of years beneath the Earth's surface as petroleum and coal into its gaseous state that we call carbon dioxide gas. This gaseous form of carbon dioxide that results from our use of fossil fuels is accumulating in the atmosphere. As carbon dioxide gas becomes more concentrated, it traps an increasing amount of the Sun's radiant (heat) energy in the Earth's atmosphere, preventing the radiant energy from escaping into space, a process that is commonly known as the greenhouse effect."

He explained, "It's called the greenhouse effect because just as the glass panes in a greenhouse prevent the Sun's radiant energy from escaping and cause the greenhouse interior to warm-up, the buildup of carbon dioxide gas in the Earth's atmosphere is causing the planet's atmosphere to warm-up. We can thank this greenhouse effect for providing us a planet warm enough to live and thrive on. However, we do not want to see the greenhouse effect become so strong that it causes a dramatically warmer atmosphere that may challenge our ability to survive."

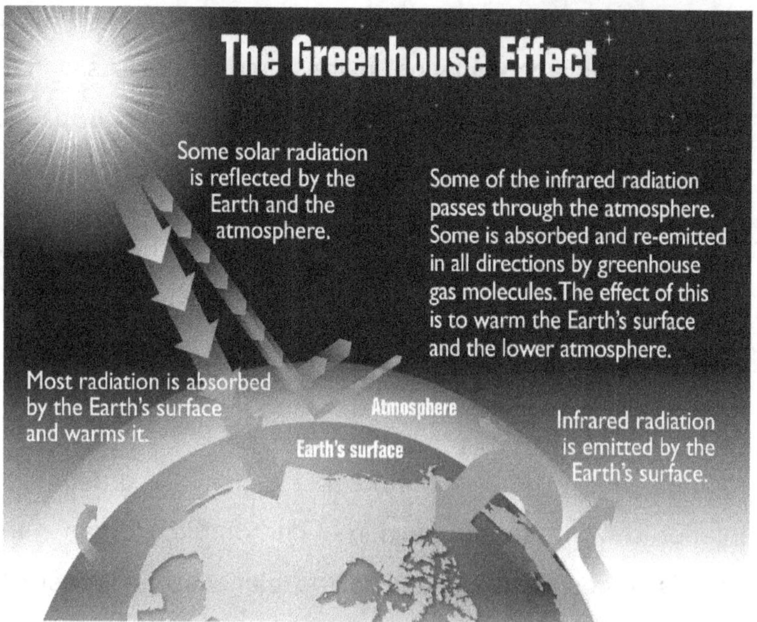

Figure 3. The Greenhouse Effect

Source: United States EPA via commons.wikimedia.org

Scott knew exactly what the Professor was talking about. He made a point of parking his car in a sunny spot during the colder months, as it was nice and warm inside by late-morning after absorbing hours of sunlight, thanks to the car's windows that trapped much of the Sun's radiant energy.

During the question and answer session at the end of the Professor's lecture, Scott asked, "What about those that say the ice core records indicate that carbon dioxide gas changes lag global temperature changes? Does this not refute the notion that the buildup of carbon dioxide gas is driving the current warming of the Earth's atmosphere?"

Professor Goodspeed responded in a pleasant yet authoritative way, "That's a question I get asked a lot." The audience murmured; an indication that many were wondering the same thing as Scott.

As the room quieted, the Professor continued, "It's one nuance in climate science that makes this problem of human-caused global warming hard for many people to grasp. As you said, scientists studying ice core samples have found that increases in carbon dioxide concentrations lag behind global temperature increases as the Earth transitions from a cold ice age state to a warm inter-glacial state like we live in today."

He cleared his throat, then continued, "To avoid making this a long technical explanation, I'll just get to the point. Ultimately, an increase in the intensity of sunlight reaching the Earth's surface and atmosphere caused by periodic changes in the Earth's orbit around the Sun is what causes an ice age to end and initiates a warming trend. However, the increase in the intensity of sunlight is not enough to drive the warming of Earth's atmosphere beyond an initial 800 to 1,000-year period coming out of an ice age. The initial increase in sunlight intensity-driven warming causes the release of carbon dioxide gas as the ice sheets melt and retreat towards the polar regions, which increases the concentration of carbon dioxide in the atmosphere. At this point the increasing concentration of carbon dioxide gas in the atmosphere takes over as the primary driver of planetary warming, driven by a positive feedback loop in which additional warming leads to additional melting of ice, which causes additional releases of carbon dioxide gas and so on until global temperatures naturally reach a plateau as an inter-glacial warm period matures and ice sheets stop melting and retreating. Eventually, approximately 10,000 to 12,000 years into a warm inter-glacial period, the Earth's orbit around the Sun changes again, which decreases the sun's intensity and the amount of sunlight reaching the Earth's surface and atmosphere, which causes the process to reverse; eventually leading to a new ice age."

The professor drank some water and took a moment to collect his thoughts, then continued, "It has been approximately 12,500 years since the last ice age ended. The ice core record indicates global temperatures were slowly dropping from an inter-glacial peak that occurred approximately 7,000 years ago. If left to its own devices, Earth would be naturally slipping into a new ice age right about now. Of course, this slide into a new ice age has been abruptly disrupted by the strong global warming temperature trend that became established during the 1980s and the global average temperature has now well surpassed the former inter-glacial peak that occurred approximately 7,000 years ago."

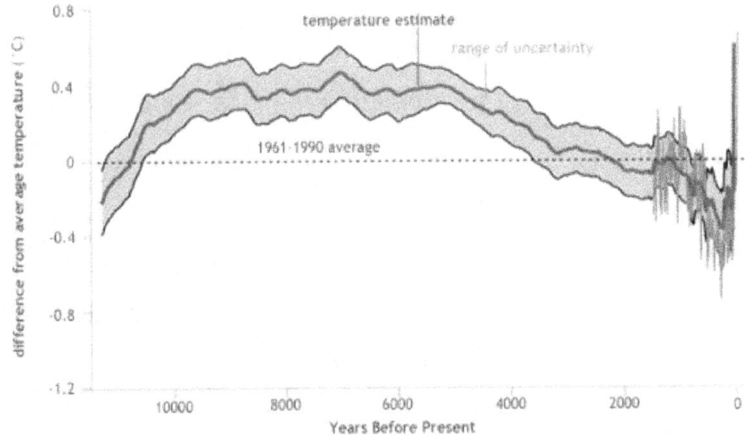

Figure 4. The Current Inter-Glacial Period

Source: United States NOAA climate.gov

He finished his explanation by saying, "Over the past two hundred years mankind has been dumping greenhouse gases into the atmosphere at a far faster rate than would naturally occur during an inter-glacial warming period. Given what we know about the past climate reactions to an increased concentration of carbon dioxide gas in Earth's atmosphere, this unnaturally fast buildup of greenhouse gases will eventually cause a violent warming response from the atmosphere. This is why so many scientists are concerned about the potential for human-caused runaway global warming in the not too distant future. The climate crisis storm clouds are gathering. The actions we take to deal with the growing climate crisis are of utmost importance if we want to live on a habitable planet."

He concluded the question and answer session by saying, "Thank you for attending my lecture about this very important topic. For additional information, please visit my website. I hope everyone has a good evening."

After the lecture, as Scott hurried back to his apartment, the sky lit up with lightning from an approaching thunderstorm. As the storm drew closer, and the thunder grew louder, it made Scott think about the approaching climate storm the Professor had just warned the audience about. Rain started pouring down just as he reached his building's entrance. As he entered, he turned around to watch the wind-driven deluge of water just outside the entrance and thought with despair, "The chances of the approaching climate storm blowing over and missing us are slim to none."

Chapter 9
Kicking the Habit

What happened over the next few months in response to the ice sheet collapsing and massive coastal flooding that ensued surprised and reassured Scott. There was no longer a way for governments to ignore the problem of global warming since the ice sheet collapse created enormous chaos and problems throughout the world and foretold of more global warming trouble ahead.

All areas previously within three meters (approximately ten feet) of sea level and connected to an ocean were under water. The flooding caused severe economic chaos and displaced over 500 million people from their homes. Stock markets around the world lost 60% of their value in a matter of weeks, as the world economy ground to a halt. It was a "green swan" event (an unexpected environmental catastrophe) that many environmentalists and economists had warned about for decades, but few believed would happen so soon. The outcry for action throughout the world was overwhelming and world leaders responded.

Instead of continuing the charade that it was too expensive to deal with global warming, governments around the world convened an emergency meeting in July 2052 at the United Nations in New York to discuss immediate measures that could be taken to address the evolving climate change crisis. As a sign of just how dire the situation was as leaders from around the world met, many of the streets around the United Nations building in New York were flooded by seawater from the nearby East River that is connected to the Atlantic Ocean via New York Harbor.

There was optimism in the air that world leaders would come to a sensible agreement to deal with the greenhouse gas emission problem. As people waited to hear the results of the United Nations emergency meeting, the successful 1987 international environmental agreement that phased out the use of ozone destroying chlorofluorocarbons (CFCs), known as The Montreal Protocol, was put forward as an example of how nations have worked together to fix an environmental problem. People around the world hoped this spirit of international cooperation would be repeated to address the climate crisis.

World leaders quickly came to an agreement to phase out contributors to global warming as quickly as possible, including fossil fuels such as oil, coal, and natural gas. Companies and consumers would be provided generous tax breaks and credits to assist them with the cost of switching to non-carbon forms of energy. Meat production was also addressed, as governments agreed to levy significant taxes on meat products to reduce their consumption and pledged to use the money to steer people towards plant-based sources of protein that had much less of a carbon footprint. A big tree-planting push was endorsed as an immediate effort to remove carbon dioxide from the air. Finally, a task force was set up to study and evaluate man-made geoengineering solutions that could be implemented on a global scale to stop and reverse global warming. However, no immediate plans were made to implement geoengineering solutions, as cost concerns and worries about unintended consequences that could result from interfering with the Earth's climate made countries wary about taking such drastic measures.

In recent decades, dwindling supplies of oil had caused the retail price of petroleum products to skyrocket. Even though replacement technologies had made a dent in fossil fuel use, the world economy still ran primarily on oil. Fossil fuels were heavily ingrained in the economic fabric of the world economy when the decision was made to end their use.

Despite the dire predictions of global warming skeptics and deniers that ending the use of fossil fuels would cause economic collapse (Scott was very familiar with such predictions since his grandfather held these views and made sure everyone knew how he felt), what followed the agreement to end the fossil fuel era and switch to clean non-carbon based energy sources turned out to be a big net positive for the world economy. The economic boom that accompanied the switch to non-carbon energy technologies was an economic surge that rarely occurs, such as the gold rushes of the 19th century, the dot.com boom of the late 20th century, or the robotics boom of the 2030s.

The switch to cheaper non-carbon sources of energy was welcomed by consumers since the new carbon-free energy technologies reduced what they paid for energy considerably. Consumers that were paying up to 20% of their income to power their vehicles and heat and cool their homes, were now paying just 2% of their income for far cheaper non-carbon-based energy technologies that were not contributing to global warming. This put a lot of money into people's pockets that they could spend on other things, which fueled economic growth for many years.

The non-carbon power sources were not only inexpensive, they were also much more stable in price than fossil fuels had been, which helped businesses make smart long-term investment decisions, further boosting economic growth. There was also a lot of work for people who designed, manufactured, and installed the new carbon-free energy technologies.

Another driver of economic growth was a huge uptick of government and private industry spending on infrastructure and other measures needed to address the reality that the infrastructure and buildings that were flooded by the sea level rise needed to be rebuilt on higher ground.

As the economy boomed, Scott settled into a routine working as a solar installer. Solar had become the preferred energy source for many home and business owners ever since Tesla, the company legendary visionary Elon Musk founded, rocked the energy world in the fall of 2052 with an inexpensive solid-state super battery array capable of storing enough energy to power a home or business for six months.

Super-efficient solar cells that could produce electricity on sunny and cloudy days combined with the Tesla super battery array meant electricity generated using solar technologies could be stored for months for use when needed. This advancement in battery technology literally made renewable energy the cheapest and most reliable energy option available. Not surprisingly, people around the world responded by purchasing solar energy systems for their home or business, relying on the Tesla super battery array or a competitor's product to provide stored electricity when needed.

The 2052 United Nations agreement to replace fossil fuels with non-carbon dioxide emitting technologies meant good times for Scott and his fellow renewable energy installers. They had more work than they could handle and opportunities to make money working overtime were ample.

The Canadian government made job retraining for fossil fuel industry workers that lost their jobs a priority. Many found work installing not only renewable energy systems but also electric vehicle charging stations and infrastructure, since the world was switching over to electric vehicles entirely because the carbon dioxide emitting internal combustion engine was being quickly phased out.

Chapter 10
Things Heat Up in California

Scott's employer, WorldWide Solar, required installers to visit their United States headquarters in the hills overlooking Santa Rosa, California for a one week training course that taught them how to install the latest 60% efficient solar tile roofs and 75% efficient solar voltaic panels. These super-efficient solar products were hot sellers since they made solar power with long-duration battery backup practical to use in just about any location, even in areas that received only modest amounts of sunlight. WorldWide Solar was eager to train their installers and Scott was happy to be one of the first Canadian installers to undergo the required training.

He hadn't been back to California since his trip around the world, but he had read a lot about the mega-state on the west coast of America and how it was experiencing many impacts from the ongoing warming of the planet. One of the biggest impacts had been the expansion of the "fire season," which used to last for a few dry summer and early fall months, but was now a problem most of the year, due to excessive heat and droughts that lasted much longer than in the past.

He caught a flight to San Francisco on a plane fueled by certified Branson synthetic aviation fuel or B-fuel for short, which was a carbon-neutral fuel derived from carbon dioxide captured from the atmosphere. The certification was named after the late Sir Richard Branson of Virgin Airlines fame who pioneered the development of the carbon-neutral synthetic aviation fuel that was used by the airline industry as a replacement for petroleum-derived jet fuel, which had been phased out by the 2052 United Nations agreement.

By the late 2030s, the airline industry's revenue was being impacted because of a growing boycott of air travel by climate activists and others concerned with the industry's carbon dioxide emissions. Sir Richard funded and oversaw the development of carbon dioxide derived synthetic aviation fuel in response to people's concerns over the aviation industry's contribution to greenhouse gas emissions and global warming.

B-fuel was produced by drawing carbon dioxide out of the air and performing a non-polluting refining process using renewable energy that resulted in a high-grade synthetic aviation fuel. Branson's B-fuel didn't gain wide acceptance until after the 2052 agreement that required the phase out of petroleum fuels, which instantly created a massive market for the carbon-neutral fuel.

During the flight, Scott read an article about how dire the Golden State's water supply problem had become due to an unusually long drought that had been ongoing for eight years. Meteorologists and climatologists blamed the record-breaking drought on a persistent high-pressure system that anchored itself in the northeastern part of the Pacific Ocean. The unusually strong and persistent high acted as a block along the west coast of the United States. It directed rainstorms away from California and the rest of the west coast, taking the much-needed rain producers into Alaska and Canada.

The pressure pattern and drought connection to climate change was clear. A persistent pool of warm water in the western Pacific associated with global warming had caused the jet stream high in the atmosphere to twist and buckle in an unusual way that allowed the massive high pressure system to form and persist off the west coast of the United States.

As a result of this pattern, California received just a third of its normal rainfall. The little rain that it received came from summer monsoon rains originating in the Southern Pacific and Mexico as well as occasional winter storms that made their way through the state when the high-pressure ridge briefly weakened.

Scientists from multiple disciplines warned that California's population centers would soon face the same fate that Cape Town, South Africa and Sydney, Australia had faced during the 2030s, when these two major cities literally ran out of water due to prolonged droughts. They recommended building massive water desalinization and purification plants powered by renewable energy to tap the Pacific Ocean waters. But their recommendations got bogged down by environmentalists who worried about using Pacific Ocean waters that had been polluted over the years with everything from industrial to radioactive waste. There was also a determined contingent of anti-tax activists that challenged any proposals that were made to address environmental problems using public funding and tied the desalinization plant proposals up in the courts.

Politicians side-stepped the issue by reassuring the restless public that rains would return in sufficient amounts to head off a total loss of water. In the article, scientists argued that such statements were not grounded in the reality of a warming world and the State of California should take measures to mitigate the effects of the prolonged drought that had no end in sight before a catastrophic loss of potable water occurred in major cities.

Scott had one of those moments when he felt angry at the lack of resolve to find a practical solution to a clearly identifiable problem. After the total chaos and significant human suffering and death tolls that Cape Town and Sydney had suffered when their cities' water supplies ran dry, he was having a hard time comprehending why people in California weren't taking the warnings seriously and putting aside their concerns to find a workable solution that everyone could live with. After all, water desalinization and purification had become commonplace and could easily deliver clean drinkable water from the Pacific Ocean using renewable energy.

He thought it was odd that environmentalists and the anti-tax crowd were taking a hard stand on such a critical issue knowing that providing public access to potable drinking water was critical to the State's survival. Universal potable drinking water was also something that made a first world country such as the United States stand out compared to third world countries that failed to provide their citizens potable drinking water either due to the cost or a lack of initiative. With exasperation he thought, "Without drinkable water, people and society can't function. There is no point in hoping that Mother Nature will help by providing miracle rainstorms. This demands a big coordinated response, like people have done many times in the past to address looming problems, not wishful thinking."

It reminded him that even in his country the Canadian government had agreed to open up Arctic regions of Canada to oil exploration and drilling during the 2040s, under intense pressure from international oil companies and ordinary people that wanted jobs and access to cheap oil. The government had to reverse its position abruptly in 2052 when petroleum exploration was banned after the ice sheet collapsed. His stomach turned as he thought about that past misstep and the water crisis unfolding in California. He thought angrily, "People can be so damn greedy and short-sighted!"

The article included a warning from scientists to the leaders of California that it was long past the time to reinstate their strict forest fire control measures that they had relaxed under corporate and public pressure a decade prior. They warned that the state could face massive firestorms that would burn populated areas and threaten humans and animals alike, similar to what Australia had experienced during the late 2010s and well into the 2020s until Australians took decisive actions to address their wildfire problem. With the ongoing drought, under-use of controlled burns, and the expansion of populations into dry wooded areas, the article concluded with an ominous warning that it was not a matter of if but when California would experience fires on a scale that it had never seen since humans populated the area.

Scott's deep thoughts and turning stomach were interrupted by the plane's Captain who said, "Flight deck here. We are beginning our descent into San Francisco International. Current weather is sunny, with a temperature of 90 degrees. It's also quite hazy because of fires burning in the east bay hills. We appreciate you flying with us today and hope we met your expectations!"

Scott had heard a lot of pilots give their pre-landing spiel, but he had never heard one mention haze due to fires in the area in which they were about to land. Hearing it didn't improve his mood, as he felt his stomach take another turn.

As the plane landed, he watched water lap up against the flood wall that had been installed to protect the airport from the bay. San Francisco had raised the whole airport by three meters (approximately ten feet) a decade ago and installed a sizable flood wall to provide further protection. The raised airport elevation and flood wall were high enough to protect the airport from the sudden sea level rise that recently occurred. However, to Scott it was an ominous sight to see bay water lapping up against the flood wall. "How long is that going to protect the airport as sea level continues to rise?" he thought.

Scott caught his self-driving electric Uber ride powered by renewable energy to his hotel near WorldWide Solar's corporate headquarters. The area he was heading to was about an hour north of San Francisco in a beautiful part of the state known as "wine country" since it boasts many wineries.

His mood improved as his driverless car made its way through the city and onto the Golden Gate Bridge. While the car crossed the world-famous bridge, he peered out over San Francisco Bay, looking at Alcatraz Prison Island and an assortment of ships moving about the bay with the San Francisco skyline as a backdrop.

As the car departed the bridge and entered Marin County, he could see the haze had thickened and it wasn't long before he spotted a couple of fires in the hills to the northwest.

To pass the time as the driverless car traveled northward, he activated Uber's conversation app on the screen in front of him. After answering a few quick questions that determined what sort of conservation he was seeking, he was engaged in a conversation with Janice, who was an artificial intelligence (AI) derived thirty-year-old woman from the San Francisco Bay Area. Her primary interests were renewable energy and climate change, which per her AI programming made her masterful at engaging in a conversation about these two topics.

Janice asked in a California accent that sounded completely natural and human, "Hi, I'm Janice. I hope you're enjoying your ride. What's your name?"

Scott answered, "Hi Janice. I'm Scott."

"So, what brings you to the Bay Area Scott?" Janice asked.

He responded, "I'm a solar installer and need to get trained on the latest technology."

After spending twenty minutes talking to his AI friend about the latest developments in solar energy technology, Scott changed the subject by asking, "Janice, how badly was the Bay Area affected by the Great Rise (the short name for the rapid three meter sea level rise) that occurred last year?"

She responded, "In the unprotected low-lying areas, it was quite bad with businesses and people's homes completely flooded. Luckily, since the rise didn't happen all at once, people had time to move out of harm's way and there was no loss of life. Also, the Bay Area had been more proactive than other parts of the country as far as preparing for the predicted sea level rise, so a lot of areas had protection. We just weren't expecting it to happen so soon."

Scott replied, "Nobody was."

She continued, "Other parts of the country weren't nearly as prepared and suffered greatly."

Eager to take advantage of her AI knowledge, he asked, "Which parts of the U.S. suffered the most from the Great Rise?"

She replied, "That would be southern Louisiana and southern Florida. Infighting among politicians over which approach to take and disagreements regarding how bad the sea level rise would be prevented the construction of many of the proposed protective sea walls. In some areas it wasn't even practical to build barriers to keep the sea out.

Unfortunately, many people ignored warnings that they lived in areas that the sea would someday reclaim. Due to the extent of the areas affected and poor communication, tens of thousands of people found themselves trapped by the rising sea and many of them died."

In a saddened voice, Scott said quietly, "Wow! That's tragic, especially because it was preventable since people could have agreed to build sea barriers or just moved out of harm's way."

She responded softly, "Yes, very tragic and unnecessary."

As the car wound through a stretch of coastal hills, it whisked through an area of smoke, the smell of which soon reached Scott's nose.

Scott snorted and said, "I'm sure it was worse in other parts of the world."

She replied humbly, "Oh yes it was. Many poor countries could not afford to build any flood protections in their low-lying coastal areas and the loss of life was a tragedy rarely seen in human history, as communication regarding the impending disaster was inadequate and many were trapped by rising water."

Scott sat silently processing what she had said when his attention was taken away from his AI friend for a few moments as the car took an exit for a local roadway towards his destination near Santa Rosa. As he looked out of the window, he could see large flames and a lot of smoke on the hillside not far to the east.

He asked Janice, "What about these fires? Is this normal for this time of the year around here?"

She replied, "Far from normal. Fire season just keeps getting longer and seemingly worse over time."

Scott was curious and asked, "What is the current fire danger threat level?"

It only took Janice a few milliseconds to scan the Internet and respond, "The area you are traveling to has an extreme fire danger threat per the National Forest Service. Experts warn that the burst of rain from an unprecedented tropical rainstorm that affected northern California a few months ago caused unusually explosive vegetation growth that has dried out and could fuel dangerous forest fires in ways that are not entirely understood."

Scott shuddered and thought, "TMI," and then responded, "It's been nice sharing the ride with you Janice. Perhaps we'll meet again in cyberspace someday."

She replied, "Nice talking to you too Scott. I hope your training goes well. Be safe!"

The app automatically turned itself off and Scott sat looking at the countryside as the car made its way to his hotel. He was relieved to see clear skies and no sign of fires when he pulled up to the hotel.

The next morning when he arrived at WorldWide Solar's headquarters for the first day of training, he sat down next to a female installer named Sarah. Being a polite Canadian, he introduced himself right away. It turned out she had recently been hired by another WorldWide Solar office in the Calgary area and was staying at his hotel.

They wound up doing much of the training together, as a lot of the installation tasks required two installers working together. They hit it off so well that it wasn't even awkward when at the end of the week of training Scott asked her if she'd be interested in joining him for dinner to celebrate their completion of the training. She accepted without pause.

They wound up going to a great Thai Restaurant in Santa Rosa, which was a real treat for both of them since good Thai food was scarce in Calgary. Afterward, they went back to their hotel lounge and had a few drinks while they watched a Calgary Flames hockey game on a holoviewer.

While two-dimensional extremely high definition televisions still existed and were still widely used in 2053, three-dimensional holoviewers had become the rage, especially when watching sporting events at a bar. The holoviewer was set up in a small stadium seating area. From their seats, Scott and Sarah could see lifelike three-dimensional renditions of the arena and hockey players as they skated, checked, and took shots at the goal on the ice in Calgary. The surround-sound system that captured the game sounds made the experience seem even more lifelike.

It was a great game that ended with Calgary beating their Vancouver rivals in overtime. It was late when the game ended. Scott was too tired from the long week of training to stay up any longer. He sensed Sarah felt tired as well. They said goodnight before retiring to their separate rooms, which weren't far from each other on the same floor of the hotel.

The combination of a long week of training and a night of entertainment put Scott to sleep quickly. He was having a nice dream about being together with Sarah back home in Calgary. On some level he was starting to have a fondness for her, which made for a pleasant dream. The kind of dream he never wanted to end.

He suddenly woke up to a frantic knock on his door and heard Sarah's screaming voice but couldn't make out what she was saying because of a loud noise outside. He was terribly groggy after being woken up from such a pleasant dream. He heard frantic knocking again, which turned into pounding and Sarah's increasingly frantic voice. He couldn't see anything going on outside due to the heavy curtain over his hotel room window, but he could hear a roar, like a windstorm was hitting the hotel.

He forced himself out of his bed and groggily stumbled to the door. As soon as he opened it, he knew from the look on Sarah's face that it was serious. She had worry lines on her forehead, a red face, and was extremely agitated, as she screamed in his face, "We have to get out of here now!"

Without asking any questions, Scott put his shoes and light jacket on as fast as he could, grabbed his wallet and phone and followed her quickly down the hallway. Many of the room's doors were wide open and only visible by emergency lighting, which creeped Scott out as they rushed by them.

As they made their way to the stairway door, he still hadn't put together in his groggy mind exactly what was going on. When Sarah opened the door to the stairway, he smelled smoke and said, "Holy moly, how close?"

As they scurried down the stairs she replied, "I don't know. I was woken up by someone pounding on my door telling me to get out and go somewhere, but I couldn't understand where. I noticed the electricity was out and heard a strange roaring sound outside. As I took a peek out of my window, I saw an orange glow and knew we had to get out of here as soon as possible. It looks like everyone else has already left."

As they approached the exit to the parking lot, they could see a bright orange glow through the small window on the door and could hear an eerie roar. As they got to the door, they didn't open it right away. The door was very hot and the view across the parking lot was a hellscape of blowing fire. They looked at each other with equally worried and baffled looks.

Scott said with trepidation in his voice, "We've got to get out of here. It's only a matter of time before…"

He was interrupted by a frantic man who bumped into him and nearly knocked him over as the man kicked the door open and ran out into the parking lot. The blast of heat and noise from the open door were overwhelming. The hot wind quickly slammed the door shut. They saw no sign of the man anywhere in the hellscape as they peered out at the parking lot.

Scott was shaken up badly. Sarah grabbed hold of him and held him. He was happy to feel her embrace. After taking a few deep breaths, Scott continued with urgency, "This place will go up in flames soon. We have to find a safe place to ride this out." He said this knowing there was nowhere he knew of in the inhospitable parking lot or anywhere nearby that would be safer than where they were at that moment.

Sarah's mind was working overtime. She remembered when her car arrived at the hotel to drop her off it had crossed a small bridge over a decent-sized drainage ditch. She forcefully took Scott's hand and said, "Follow me!"

Before Scott could say, "Where?" she had already kicked the door open and was leading him outside. They were greeted by an incredible roar and searing heat from the wall of fire across the parking lot. She quickly guided Scott around the corner of the hotel to the front area. Although there was fire all around, the front side was shielded from the strong winds that were fanning the fire, providing a respite from the intense heat and noise. Scott felt a bit of relief as Sarah quickly led him across the hotel's front parking lot and into the drainage ditch.

They weren't the only ones who had taken refuge in the ditch. It was deep enough to provide good cover from the firestorm that surrounded the hotel. Luckily, it was made of concrete, so there are no concerns about dry vegetation catching fire.

The hotel manager was pacing the ditch checking on guests. As he approached them, he asked, "Are you okay?"

Sarah said, "I guess. We're pretty shaken, but relieved to be out of the hotel and here in the ditch."

The hotel manager nodded and looked up at the hotel, drawing their attention to the building. The top floors on the backside of the hotel where they had been sleeping just a few minutes before had caught fire.

Sarah was very concerned. She asked the manager, "What happened to the fire alarm?"

He replied, "We lost power shortly before the fire headed towards the hotel. The winds changed direction and the fire quickly picked up speed. It must have raced five miles towards the hotel in under a half an hour based on where it was earlier this evening. That happens sometimes in these hills, as local factors create their own environment during these wildfires, and they spread extremely quickly. The fire must have taken out the power and our backup power failed, so we had no alarm. My assistant and I ran through the hotel, pounding on doors, alerting guests to get out and go to the front ditch. The hotel was only one-half full. Given all the people in this ditch, I think everyone got out in time. If it gets more intense, you can take shelter under the bridge."

Sarah held Scott tightly as she asked, "Where are the fire fighter crews?"

The manager replied, "There are so many fires burning in California right now that they are spread thinly and are trying to protect more populated areas. If this dies down by morning, they'll make their way up here in the hills to check on us."

Holding Scott closely, she asked, "I guess you've been through this before?"

The manager said, "I grew up in these hills. Yes, I've been through this several times, but it's happening more often, and the fires are growing more intense. I have to wonder how much longer people will be able to live up here if this keeps up. Anyway, let me know if you need anything, I have to check on the others."

Scott and Sarah held each other as they watched the hotel burn to the ground revealing the burnt hills behind the former hotel. Eventually the fire calmed down, and they fell asleep in the concrete ditch.

Scott and Sarah woke up in the morning to the commotion of fire personnel and rescue workers helping people out of the ditch and checking on their well-being. They were transported to a Red Cross shelter in Santa Rosa where they had a few snacks and wiped their faces, arms, and legs, which had been covered in an ash-laden grimy material from the fire. To get a proper shower and a good night's sleep, they spent the night at a local hotel in the city.

A self-driving electric Uber car picked them up the following morning and took them to San Francisco International Airport. Unlike his trip to Santa Rosa, Scott had a real woman to talk to on the way to the airport. They were both in a bit of shock knowing that they could have lost their lives in the fire, so they kept their conversation light.

Scott was able to get them seats next to each other on the flight home to Calgary. They finally felt relaxed and had a conversation about what had happened.

By the time they were ready to say goodbye in the airport he felt a strong connection to her. They had been through so much together over the past two days. As they said their goodbyes and held each other, he felt like he never wanted to let go. He finally let go of her and they stood looking at each other. He was not sure what to do next. She sensed he was feeling awkward about asking for her phone number, so she asked for his and texted her number to him. He saw her get into an Uber and waved goodbye.

His head was spinning as he thought about what had transpired over the past forty-eight hours. Not just the frightful experience, but that he connected with a woman romantically for the first time in his life. It wasn't as if he was trying to avoid romantic connections; it was just that dating wasn't a high priority for him since he had moved to Calgary and he never made much of an effort in that regard. This was such a random and spontaneous romantic interlude in his relatively monotonous life that he was having a hard time processing what had just happened as he stood in front of the airport.

His train of thought was broken by his phone buzzing repeatedly in his pocket. The driverless Uber had arrived, and it appeared that it was growing impatient with its customer that was standing on the sidewalk in a daze. He laughed a bit and thought, "Do these AI cars have emotions these days?"

On the way back to his apartment, he used Uber's conversation app to chat with an AI female named Louise that was about Sarah's age. He wanted to know all about love and how to have a successful relationship. He was amazed and a bit confused at how quickly his bond with Sarah had developed and was desperate for guidance.

He told his AI friend the circumstances of his suddenly found romantic interest. Louise explained to him that it was not uncommon for two people that experience a life-threatening situation together to wind up with a romantic bond afterward. The unintended excitement surrounding such an experience mimics the brain chemicals that are released within the body as people fall in love. The romantic bond is reinforced by the fact that they survived the life-threatening experience together.

During the forty-five-minute car ride, he noted all of his AI friend's advice and thanked her as the car pulled up to his apartment building.

Chapter 11
A Walk in the Park

Being back in Calgary brought Scott back to the reality that not all that long ago the world had taken a big step towards a global warming apocalypse with the sudden rise of sea level around the world. This reality was reinforced by the unusually strong fire season he had unfortunately just experienced during his job training visit to California. It was a disturbing reality to face, but he knew he had to press on, perform his job, and remain active in the movement to address the climate crisis.

He was eager to get in touch with Sarah, but he knew from the AI friend he had consulted on the way back from the airport that a guy doesn't want to appear desperate or easy to get to a woman that he's interested in dating. There's an unspoken ritual that is followed in which a guy plays a game of hard to get to increase the desire in his romantic interest.

The more he thought about it, the more ridiculous it seemed as far as his potential relationship with Sarah was concerned. It's not as if they hadn't already shared a big life experience together that bonded them in a special way. He concluded, "Given the circumstances, there is no unspoken ritual that needs to be followed."

When he got home from work Friday evening, he called her up. She was happy to hear from him and was wondering what took him so long to call. He blamed it on being busy catching up at work. He was too tired to meet up that evening after the recent travel and long work week; a feeling Sarah shared. She took the lead and set up a date to meet for coffee at her favorite downtown coffeehouse the following morning.

Scott watched people pass by the window of the coffeehouse as he waited for her inside Eco Roasters in downtown Calgary. He was a bit nervous about seeing her again. The past two weeks had been a whirlwind, and he had to be honest with himself, despite their great working relationship during the training, nice dinner together, and sincere romantic interaction during and after their frightening fire experience, he really didn't know her. He calmed himself by focusing on how exciting it would be to get to know more about her and let his mind wander as he imagined what she would tell him about her outlook on life.

She texted him she was running a few minutes late, so he picked up a menu and read Eco Roasters' mission on the back.

"Eco Roasters is a proud member of the growing net-zero carbon movement. We have integrated policies into

our business practices that have eliminated all carbon dioxide releases. We ensure that our suppliers are certified net-zero carbon businesses and adhere to international fair-trade principals. We also dedicate 10% of our profits to organizations working towards a cleaner greener sustainable future."

"Cool! I have to read about this net-zero carbon thing," Scott thought.

As he looked up, he could see her making her way into the coffeehouse. He was pleasantly surprised as she had made herself up and looked stunning. He wasn't expecting this and blushed because he looked more like he had just rolled out of bed on a Saturday, although he had taken a shower.

His apprehension soon dissipated as she reached the table, and he got up to give her a hug. It all seemed so natural as they embraced and shared a hearty hug. There was no awkwardness between them.

"It's great to see you! You look fabulous!" he said with sincere enthusiasm.

She responded with equal enthusiasm, "You too! Let's get some coffee!" and smiled.

When they returned to their table with large lattes in hand, Scott said, "So, what got you involved in working as a solar installer?"

She replied, "Well, my family moved to Alberta years ago, so my dad could work in the oil tar sands. It was some of the best money to be had in Canada at the time."

Scott nodded, as he knew that from his grandfather who was adamant about protecting oil tar sands jobs.

She continued, "I guess it was good for me and my older brother, as we weren't wanting for anything growing up, but we also lost our dad before I turned twenty and I couldn't help but blame his illness on the work he did. It paid well, but it was very unhealthy. After he passed away, I felt that I wanted to dedicate my life to working to promote a cleaner form of energy for future generations, so people didn't have to lose a parent due to unhealthy oil related work. I entered a solar installer training program offered by the Province and here I am today, an installer with three years of experience under my belt."

Scott thought about what she said and responded with concern in his voice, "That's touching Sarah. I'm so sorry you lost your father so young."

She replied, "Yeah, he was a great dad, and it was sad to lose him so young, but his death has given me a purpose in life. This might sound odd since you don't really know me, but sometimes I feel like he's still with me guiding me to make the right decisions. I feel like he helped guide me in making my decision to become a solar installer." They looked at each other for a few moments as she reflected about her father and he thought about what she said. She then asked, "How about you?"

Scott told her about his background growing up in the Yukon being raised in large part by his old-school grandfather. He told her about his life-changing trip around the world in which he witnessed some early signs of global warming's impacts and the preparations being made by cities and countries around the world before the great sea level rise occurred. How it was during that trip he decided to work in an industry that is helping to prevent a future climate disaster. He finished by saying, "Solar is playing such an important role in reducing our emissions of carbon dioxide that I knew being an installer of a net-zero carbon energy source like solar was exactly what I wanted to do."

She admired that he was driven by a noble purpose to be a solar installer, even though they were motivated to choose their career for different reasons.

They had lunch at the coffeehouse that included a lengthy discussion about climate change issues, which she was not as up to date on as he was but was eager to learn more about. They also talked about the harrowing experience they went through in California a little over a week ago. At one point he took her hand and thanked her for leading him out of the hotel to safety. She blushed, knowing they had formed a lifelong bond as they escaped the fire together.

It was a beautiful day in Calgary, so after eating they continued their impromptu date with a walk through a park. Upon completing a lengthy walk which included discussions about lighter topics, such as what television shows they liked and what their favorite kind of food was, they bought some ice cream and sat down on a bench that overlooked a pond.

With his mind racing from the exuberance of spending the day with Sarah, he asked a question that in hindsight was a bit too forward given they had just met. He asked, "With the ever-expanding world population being one of the primary drivers of global warming, what do you think about having children?"

She looked a bit shocked at the question, but not overly so. She already knew him well enough to know that the climate crisis was often at the fore of his mind, so wrote it off as an innocent question.

Scott sensed her surprise at his question and felt a bit embarrassed as he thought, "That was a stupid question to ask!"

Not wanting to ruin what had been a fantastic date, she set aside her surprise and answered, "You know, I haven't really thought about it much. I know there's a growing movement of people concerned about the climate crisis vowing to forego having children. But I've never been a part of that movement and haven't really given it much thought at all. What about you?"

Scott, relieved that she answered the question nonchalantly, answered her uneasily, "I, I, I actually have never been in a serious relationship." He blushed strongly, and she blushed a bit in response with a look of surprise at his statement. He struggled to finish, "I guess in principle I admire the people who have vowed not to have children as a necessary response to prevent the climate crisis. But then I also wonder what's the point of trying to prevent the climate crisis if there are no future generations that will benefit from our actions? I guess I really don't know what I think about it."

She lightened the conversation by saying with a smile, "No worries. We don't have to solve the world's problems this afternoon," which elicited a smile from Scott.

He felt better getting it out that she was the first woman that he'd had a relationship with. They moved on to less esoteric topics like their favorite kind of movies. She liked dramatic movies, while he enjoyed climate-fiction and science-fiction movies (sometimes one and the same). She suggested they meet up that evening to see a dramatic science fiction movie that had received great reviews. He agreed that it was a good idea. They briefly hugged and said goodbye.

He was on cloud nine as he walked home from their date thinking about Sarah and all that had transpired since they had met.

Chapter 12
Getting on With Life

Scott was very disturbed by the climate events that had unfolded and he, like many others, was grasping to make sense of what had occurred with the ice sheet collapse and was wondering what Mother Nature had in store for humanity as the planet reacted to two centuries of greenhouse gases accumulating in its atmosphere. There was a significant uptick in the number of people attending religious services and seeking the advice of spiritual advisers looking for greater meaning to life. Many took an interest in politics and the social movement to address what had now become a full-on climate crisis that could no longer be denied by even the most dug-in skeptics and deniers. Sadly, there was also an uptick in drug and alcohol abuse, as some people started to lose hope in the future.

Scott found an escape by focusing on his blossoming relationship with Sarah. His life was busier than ever with his role as her boyfriend helping to keep his mind from over-fixating on the climate crisis. When he wasn't with Sarah, he spent much of his time working out at the gym or doing things outdoors, including an occasional survivalist weekend in the back country with a group from Calgary. He used quiet time during the evening to read about developments concerning the unfolding climate crisis and the growing movement to address it.

He and Sarah both loved the outdoors and were lucky to live within a few hours of one of the wonders of the world, the Canadian Rockies. Their favorite weekend outing was a visit and hike at Yoho or Jasper National Park in the Rockies on a Saturday. They would then continue on what was perhaps the most beautiful highway in the world, the Icelands Parkway, which wound its way through the picturesque Rockies to the small town of Jasper. They would spend Saturday night in Jasper at a hotel or bed and breakfast, then spend a leisurely day on Sunday as they made their way back to Calgary that included a hike or a stop in the tourist town Banff for a meal.

They had been dating for three years when he suggested they spend a weekend at Lake Louise in the Rockies. It was a spot they had visited in passing but had never fully explored.

The beautiful emerald colored lake featured a grand hotel at one end that was built by the Canadian Pacific Railroad two centuries prior to encourage people to ride its trains that passed through the Rockies, as it offered a spectacular destination for travelers. A mountain rose at the other end of the lake which only a decade ago was capped with a glacier that used to make an ominous rumbling noise as it slowly melted and collapsed. The mountain was now barren during much of the year with only seasonal winter snows whitening its peak. A trail ran along the lake offering beautiful views of the lake, the grand hotel, and the mountain at the end of the lake. The trail continued up the mountain as it wound its way through evergreen trees and boulder-laden clearings to a small snack chalet near the top of the mountain.

After spending the night at the grand hotel, Scott and Sarah set out to hike to the snack chalet that overlooks Lake Louise. As the elevation of the trail increased, the backdrop of the breathtaking Canadian Rockies emerged in all its glory with the beautiful lake in the foreground below.

Just before they got to the chalet, Sarah stopped and turned towards the lake to take pictures of the scenery that was so beautiful it literally took her breath away for a few moments. As she took in the scenery and snapped photos, Scott fumbled around in his bag to find his water.

When she turned around, he was down on one knee holding a small velvet box in his right hand. She gasped and put her hand over her mouth.

With joy and confidence, he said, "Ever since that night we survived the wildfire in California together, I knew you were the person I wanted to spend the rest of my life with. I want you to accept this ring as our engagement to be married."

She jumped on him and kissed him saying, "Of course, of course, of course." She put the ring on. He took out a small bottle of champagne and two glasses from his bag, then poured champagne. They held each other for a long time as they sipped champagne and took in the heavenly view that lay in front of them. All their worries in the world disappeared as they took in the majesty that is the Canadian Rockies and thought about their future together.

Chapter 13
A Special Month

Scott and Sarah tied the knot in May 2057 in a ceremony overlooking Lake Louise. In keeping with their principles of wanting to minimize their impact on the climate they kept their wedding small with only close family and friends attending. Small weddings had become more common by the middle of the 21st century, as people tried to eliminate excesses in their lives.

While Scott and Sarah had a traditional gift registry that included things they needed for their apartment, they also included an option for people who would rather provide a gift that aligned with their goals in life. They asked for donations to their favorite charity that helped poor people around the world with the cost of installing solar energy. There were still places in the world that had no access to electricity. This charity's mission was to make limitless solar energy available to all, regardless of their ability to afford it.

It turned out to be a lively talking point at the wedding, as friends and relatives were curious about the solar charity and how it worked. They were happy to explain that the charity provided money to buy solar equipment and provided people to install the equipment on poor people's homes in many countries around the world, including Canada. Once installed, the solar equipment provided the beneficiaries with free solar generated electricity that resulted in a lasting improvement in their lives.

The following day they were on their way to Auckland, New Zealand to start their month-long honeymoon. Auckland was a city that had been affected substantially by the great sea level rise that occurred five years prior to their arrival. The airport had been flooded and was out of operation for a year. They landed on a newly constructed runway that had been built using fill that was placed on top of the submerged runway.

After spending a rather restless night as they tried to adjust to the significant time change, they set out on foot to see the city.

Sarah had never been to the Southern Hemisphere and felt a bit off as they walked around the city the following morning. Scott asked, "What's wrong sweets? Feeling jet-lagged?"

She replied, "I don't know? I feel a bit disoriented. I feel like the Sun should be on the south side of the sky, but it's in the north. It's throwing me off."

Scott smiled, "I know. I felt that way when I visited Australia a few years back. It's not something you think about living in the northern hemisphere your whole life. You don't even think twice that the sun is always in the southern sky, and then suddenly you're here in the southern hemisphere and it's like your equilibrium is thrown off because the sun is in the northern sky. Don't worry, it'll pass."

She felt reassured and smiled at him.

Most of the city's low-lying parts had been raised and rebuilt since the Great Rise flooded them. One block along the waterfront was left submerged under water and was coupled with a climate change learning center that overlooked it to serve as a reminder of the real and devastating consequences of the Earth's unnatural temperature increase.

As they gazed at the submerged city block from the learning center's deck, she took hold of his hand and said, "What a great idea. We can try to tell future generations about how bad the great sea level rise was, but this really brings its terrible destruction to life for all to see."

They spent the better part of two weeks touring New Zealand, seeing its incredible beauty that rivals any place of natural beauty in the world. They especially enjoyed a scenic hike that took them up a valley that contained what remained of the Tasman Glacier. The rapidly disappearing glacier had lost 75% of its mass over the past 200 years and was expected to cease to exist by the end of the 21st century as global warming continued to eat away at it.

The next leg of their honeymoon included a hop across the western Pacific to Sydney, Australia. As they toured the Sydney area, Scott remembered places he had visited along Sydney Harbor before the Great Rise that were now under water. It was a bit hard for him to comprehend how quickly things had changed.

After spending a couple of days seeing the sights in Sydney and the surrounding area, they flew to the state of Tasmania, which is an Australian island that is located south of the continent.

Since they were in the southern hemisphere, the season in early June was late fall and it felt like it in Tasmania with cold nights and cool brisk weather during the daytime. Luckily, the weather was predicted to be fair during their visit, as the late fall can be a stormy time in this part of the world.

They took advantage of the good weather and went on several hikes in the abundant national parks on the island. Their favorite hike was to the Wineglass Bay overlook in Freycinet National Park, which made for a perfect spot to picnic and take in the scenery.

As they lay in bed early in the morning on the day of their departure from Tasmania their hotel room shook for several seconds, which concerned both of them quite a lot. It turned out they had experienced their first earthquake.

While Tasmania occasionally had minor earthquakes in the past, they learned that earthquakes were occurring more frequently in recent years. Local seismologists attributed the recent uptick in earthquake activity to the melting ice sheets to the south in Antarctica. As the ice sheets melted, the Earth's crust reacted to the reduced weight load and the release of pressure, which produced strong earthquakes more frequently along the margin of the Antarctic plate than in the past when the climate was stable. Some quakes were strong enough that they could be felt as far away as Tasmania.

After flying into Sydney, they caught an overnight maglev train to Brisbane in Queensland. Their final destination was the Great Barrier Reef. Sarah had always wanted to see the famous reef that was known for its incredible beauty. Scott was eager to see the progress made in restoring the reef to its former glory since he had last visited it during his trip around the world.

Sarah rested her head on Scott's shoulder. As they both looked out of the window at the passing Australian countryside that was slightly illuminated by a half-moon, something in the sky caught Sarah's attention.

She said, "What's that?"

Scott, who was dozing off, replied softly, "What's? What?"

She said, "That!" and pointed at a star formation in the distinct shape of a cross.

As Scott focused in on what she was pointing out, he replied, "Oh, that's the Southern Cross. It's brilliant isn't it? Something we never see in Canada."

She replied, "It sure is" and squeezed a little closer to him.

They both fell asleep as they watched the Southern Cross in the night sky while the train rocked gently through curves as it made its way up the east coast of Australia.

They spent a day and night in Brisbane, enjoying the local culture and beautiful beaches. The next afternoon they caught an overnight train to Cairns, Queensland, which is in a tropical region along the northeast coast of Australia. Cairns would serve as their base as they explored the Arlington Reef, which is one of many reefs that collectively comprise the Great Barrier Reef.

After checking into their hotel, they had lunch and explored Cairns a bit. The highlight of their afternoon was an excursion to Kuranda Koala Gardens to see and cuddle koalas. Late in the day they set out to visit to a marina which had boats that took tourists out to the reef. Their Lonely Planet app recommended a boat called "Siberian Khatru" that was known to be a particularly lively and entertaining boat to ride out to the reef for a day of snorkeling, food, and drinks.

As they approached the boat to speak to a crewmember about how to get on the next day's excursion, Scott had an odd feeling about the guy who was unloading equipment from the boat. He seemed familiar to him. "How odd," he thought as they approached.

The crewmember looked up and said in a friendly voice, "How can I help you?"

Scott again was struck with the familiarity of the guy standing in front of him and said, "You wouldn't happen to have space for tomorrow's tour, eh?"

The crewmember looked Scott up and down. Scott stood looking at him with a bit of disbelief, still unaware on a conscious level of who he was. The crewmember's face suddenly brightened considerably as he said, "If it isn't my old mate Scott from the Outback! I'll never forget that Yukon accent!" and put his hand out.

Sarah had a puzzled look on her face as she looked at the crewmember and then back at Scott as they shook hands.

The realization then hit Scott all at once as he shook the crewmember's hand, "Noah! How are you? What are you doing here?"

Noah smiled and said, "I got tired of living in the bone-dry Outback with the tumbleweed and snakes. After the Great Rise, I felt a calling to work by the ocean to do something to help restore our Great Barrier Reef. The excursions help raise people's awareness of the challenges the reef faces as the ocean warms. I also spend some of my spare time as a volunteer on the reef restoration project."

Scott said, "That's awesome Noah! I didn't expect to see anyone I had met on my previous trip down under."

Noah replied with a smile, "Yeah, it's a small world isn't it. Anyway, we do have space for tomorrow."

Scott was a bit befuddled and said, "Oh, sorry this is my wife Sarah. We're actually on our honeymoon."

Sarah put her hand out and shook Noah's hand saying, "Pleasure meeting you."

Noah replied, "The pleasure is all mine. I'll put you down on the list for tomorrow's trip to the reef. Be here at 8 a.m. sharp. We'll make it a honeymoon special tomorrow!"

Scott and Sarah laughed and thanked him.

The trip out to the Great Barrier Reef the next morning was amazing, as they took in the ocean air and chatted with others who had traveled from around the world to see the wonder of nature.

As they approached the reef and prepared to snorkel, the Captain gave a brief speech, "Enjoy your time as you witness one of our most beautiful treasures. We've brought you out to a section of reef that has been a focal point of the national restoration efforts to bring the reef back from the brink. A few years back, this section was ten meters below the surface, but after the Great Rise it is now thirteen meters under the surface." People on the boat murmured as they discussed the oddity of the ocean being three meters higher than it had been just a few years ago. The Captain continued, "Enjoy your time, but please if you are one of our guests doing a dive to see the reef up close, do not stand on it or try to take a piece home. When you're done, enjoy some shrimp on the barbie and other delicious foods that our crew is preparing."

The reef did not disappoint. Snorkeling hand in hand above the restored reef and seeing the vivid assortment of colorful fish and other aquatic creatures wound up being the highlight of their honeymoon. After they finished and had a bite to eat, they enjoyed a lively conversation with Noah and some other guests from around the world as they sipped wine and enjoyed the ocean breeze while the boat headed back into the marina.

They had planned on wrapping up their honeymoon with a two-night stopover in Hong Kong. However, it had become apparent that visiting Hong Kong would not be possible. The city was on lockdown, and no flights were departing or arriving.

As the train pulled out of Cairns, Scott asked his iPhone 40 for an update on the unfolding situation in Hong Kong. Siri responded, "Hong Kong is experiencing a virus-caused epidemic that appears to have originated from a scientist who had travelled from Antarctica to the city to make a presentation at a science conference. The epidemic started just three weeks ago and has already infected approximately 50,000 people, with a mortality rate of 30%. Within three days of the outbreak, an early warning epidemic monitoring artificial intelligence program alerted health officials about detection of an unknown virus and illness cluster that had a high potential to become an epidemic. To avoid a world-wide pandemic, Hong Kong authorities quickly implemented the World Health Organization's isolation protocol that required the city to be immediately sealed off from the outside world."

Scott was very concerned at learning this. Sarah could see that and shared his concerned. Scott asked Siri, "How could a virus spread that quickly and have such an unprecedentedly high mortality rate?" Scott had an idea what the answer would be but waited for Siri.

Siri responded, "Scientists matched the virus to one that was catalogued from ice sheets in Antarctica. It is a virus that had been frozen in the ice sheets for millions of years. Humans had never been infected by it previously. The scientist apparently became infected in Antarctica as he was conducting research but wasn't experiencing symptoms until two days after he arrived in Hong Kong. Before he became sick, the scientist attended a large reception marking the opening of the conference at which he exposed thousands of people to the novel virus. Since humans do not have any natural immunity to this ancient virus that they have never encountered, it spread quickly through the city's population and has been very deadly."

Sarah jumped in with concern in her voice, "Siri, what are the chances that it will affect Australia or Canada?"

Siri responded, "The artificial intelligence program's early warning and quick implementation of the World Health Organization's isolation protocol by city officials appears to have kept the virus contained mainly in Hong Kong. A vaccine has already been developed. It passed the World Health Organization's rapid recon effectiveness and safety tests several days ago and is being administered to those who recently visited Hong Kong and others that may have been exposed. There is a 0.005% chance that this virus will cause a world-wide pandemic."

Sarah and Scott both breathed a sigh of relief. She turned to him and said, "Thankfully, we live in a time when advancements in health sciences have made addressing these deadly epidemics so quick and effective."

Scott replied, "Yeah, as bad as things are now with global warming, we have a lot to be thankful for living in this day and age. Let's make the best of the rest of our honeymoon by spending the rest of our time in Sydney. We can do the boat tour of Sydney Harbor that we didn't get a chance to go on." She snuggled with him as they watched the scenery roll by.

Chapter 14
Optimism Reigns

The results of the 2052 United Nations agreement were very impressive. By 2060, the atmospheric carbon dioxide level measured at Mauna Loa Observatory in Hawaii stabilized at a level near 550 parts per million (ppm); an encouraging development, yet still a dangerously high level. This marked the first time in 100 years of measurements that level of carbon dioxide in the atmosphere had stopped increasing and had stabilized.

With the world experiencing strong economic growth and the carbon dioxide problem being addressed, optimism reigned among most people world-wide, with a feeling that the worst of the climate crisis had been averted.

Scientists warned that such optimism was misplaced, since a lot of carbon dioxide had been released into the atmosphere over the past 200 years and it would persist at high levels for thousands of years, causing global warming to continue for the foreseeable future. They explained that carbon dioxide is removed from the atmosphere by several natural processes such as tree growth that takes decades and rock weathering that takes several thousand years to naturally remove the greenhouse gas. In other words, it would take a very long time for atmospheric carbon dioxide to naturally recede to a level at which it did not continue to cause a dangerous upward trend in global temperatures.

Many scientists recommended implementing proactive man-made geoengineering measures to reduce the carbon dioxide level in the atmosphere and to block sunlight. However, with the carbon dioxide situation stabilized, their recommendations did not receive much public or political support. It was back to business as usual for the majority of people and politicians who focused on matters other than the Earth's climate.

It had been approximately 25 million years since Earth had an atmospheric carbon dioxide concentration of 550 ppm; a time long before mankind existed. At that time, Earth experienced a very warm spell with average global temperatures 2 to 4 degrees Celsius (4 to 7 degrees Fahrenheit) warmer than they were in the 2060. During this past warm period, polar regions were largely free of ice and sea level was many meters higher than the era in which Scott and Sarah were living. With this in mind, scientists warned that with the carbon dioxide level around 550 ppm, severe impacts should be expected in coming decades and centuries, as the Earth's climate reacted to the carbon dioxide loaded into its climate system.

Scientists' warnings were made evident during the early 2060s because even though the carbon dioxide concentration in the atmosphere had stabilized, average global temperature continued its upward trajectory. As predicted, Earth's atmosphere continued to react to the elevated carbon dioxide concentration by continuing to warm and was expected to do so for the foreseeable future.

Chapter 15
Hope Springs Eternal

By the mid-2060s, the Earth's atmosphere continued to warm and the level of carbon dioxide in the atmosphere began to once again increase slightly, as the ongoing warming caused carbon dioxide releases from natural sources such as melting tundra, glaciers, and polar ice sheets to accumulate in the atmosphere.

By this time, it was clear humans could no longer sit back and wait for the Earth to heal itself. Proactive measures, well beyond anything mankind had tried in the past, were needed to stop the rising global carbon dioxide concentration and temperature trends in an effort to head off the worsening climate impacts being felt around the world. As a result, a worldwide consensus formed around an understanding that to address the impacts of global warming and climate change, more needed to be done than what was agreed to at the historic 2052 United Nations emergency meeting.

Scientists working in various disciplines at research institutions around the world had investigated geoengineering solutions for years that might reverse the underlying causes of global warming. However, their proposals were far-flung and, in most cases, unproven in real-world situations, certainly not on a large scale. Most importantly, implementing their grand solutions lacked the international consensus that was needed to fund and implement large-scale climate geoengineering schemes.

This all changed around late 2065 and early 2066, as the warming planet continued to wreak havoc on the environment and people around the world grew very concerned about what the eventual outcome of the ongoing warming would be, especially with atmospheric the carbon dioxide level rising again.

In an effort to head off runaway global warming, the 2066 Climate Geoengineering Summit convened. The summit included representatives from countries throughout the world who discussed geoengineering solutions that could be implemented to stop and reverse the upward carbon dioxide and temperature trends.

Paris was chosen for the 2066 Climate Geoengineering Summit due to its symbolic importance as the location of the first international climate summit and agreement that was finalized fifty years earlier in 2016. The climate agreement that the United States infamously left in 2020 after a global warming denying President from the early 21st century named Donald Trump decided that the world's largest economy at the time (by the 2060s the U.S. ranked #3 behind China and India) would not participate in worldwide efforts to reduce carbon dioxide emissions to a level that would keep global warming in check. Without the largest economy in the world leading the effort, the Paris climate agreement wasn't nearly as effective as it could have been and ultimately proved to be ineffective at reducing global greenhouse gas emissions significantly enough to stop the Earth from warming.

The President's decision turned out to be terribly misplaced and short-sighted given the events that unfolded in the decades that followed. It certainly hurt his legacy tremendously, as he was remembered with scorn by those suffering from the effects of climate change and a world population concerned about the future of mankind in a continuously warming greenhouse Earth.

The 2066 Climate Geoengineering Summit resulted in the formation of an international committee of stakeholders that would decide which geoengineering solutions should be pursued on a global scale. The committee included government officials from all continents, non-government organization (NGO) representatives, scientists, engineers, environmentalists, business representatives, and entrepreneurs. The committee which was known as the International Climate Change Mitigation Committee (ICCMC), was specifically tasked with evaluating and making recommendations to world leaders regarding which geoengineering solutions should be implemented to stop and eventually reduce global warming. The committee's evaluation criteria included: effectiveness at reducing carbon dioxide in the atmosphere or reducing sunlight, cost to implement, difficulty of implementation, potential for disruption to human activities, and an assessment of risks to Earth's climate and environment because of possible unintended consequences.

The committee would meet on a semi-annual basis to share their findings. They were tasked with providing a final decision by December 31, 2069 regarding which technology or combination of technologies would be recommended for implementation on a planet-wide scale. Although the problem was urgent, the world leaders that formed the committee understood that committee members would require several years to properly assess the various technologies under consideration and their overall impacts. Tinkering with the Earth's climate was not something they wanted to do without first taking the time to properly examine the available options and weigh the risks.

The final decision regarding how to proceed would require a consensus of three-quarters of the world's countries via a vote at the United Nations. The consensus was set at only three-quarters instead of requiring all countries to agree because world leaders realized that large-scale climate geoengineering approaches would likely have trouble gaining unanimous approval, which would prevent the urgent need to move forward with the recommended solutions given the worsening climate crisis. The crisis facing humanity was too great a risk to take a chance that mitigative action would be delayed by disagreements and infighting among world leaders.

As the 2060s wore on, Scott spent much of his free time reading about developments during the semi-annual ICCMC deliberations. As an eternal optimist, he had a keen interest in reading about proposed geoengineering solutions to the climate crisis. He found the various proposals interesting to read about and was eagerly awaiting the committee's final recommendations to world leaders at the end of the decade.

Scott felt fascinated to be alive, witnessing history in the making as humans grappled with solutions to the climate crisis. It reminded him of stories his grandfather had told him about watching the Berlin Wall crumble live on television in 1989, as communism in Eastern Europe fell apart. Scott now knew how his grandfather must have felt back then, as history was unfolding in front of his eyes every day, an amazing and humbling feeling.

The committee ultimately evaluated six climate geoengineering solutions. Three of the solutions involved active removal of carbon dioxide from the atmosphere. These solutions included:

Ocean Fertilization – Add iron to oceans so single cell algae called phytoplankton increase considerably in numbers. The phytoplankton use photosynthesis to grow and capture carbon from carbon dioxide in the process. Upon death, phytoplankton sink to the bottom of the oceans taking the carbon they stored with them, making the ocean bottoms carbon sinks that would hold carbon safely away from the atmosphere for a very long time.

Carbon Removal Via Filtering – Filter carbon dioxide out of the atmosphere using large-scale filtering and capture technology. The captured carbon dioxide would be used in a variety of ways from enhancing the growth environment in food-producing greenhouses to producing synthetic fuels to making carbon rock material that would lock away carbon in its solid state for millions of years.

Reforestation – Plant hundreds of billions of trees that would naturally remove carbon dioxide from the atmosphere via photosynthesis, locking away carbon within the trees. The biggest problem would be finding the land area needed to plant enough trees to be effective at removing enough carbon dioxide to make a difference. Some estimates by scientists concluded an area the size of Canada would have to be planted with trees for this geoengineering solution to be effective, which is a lot of space. The recommendation included using carbon-neutral renewable energy to pump water into arid areas to grow healthy trees.

Two of the solutions involved limiting sunlight from reaching the Earth's lower atmosphere and surface. These solutions included:

Injection of Aerosols into The Upper Atmosphere – Tiny particles called aerosols are naturally injected high up into the Earth's atmosphere by volcanoes. High concentrations of aerosols in the upper atmosphere after a major volcanic eruption have a proven cooling effect on the planet since they limit the amount of sunlight reaching the lower atmosphere and the Earth's surface. This proposal called for the injection of huge quantities of man-made aerosols into the Earth's upper atmosphere to limit the sun's heating power in the lower atmosphere and on the Earth's surface.

Deployment of Giant Mirrors in Space – Construction of giant mirrors that would be placed in space above Earth. Such mirrors would prevent some sunlight from reaching the Earth's atmosphere and surface by reflecting sunlight back into space. They would have a cooling effect on Earth's atmosphere and surface temperatures. The main drawback to this approach is that it would be extremely expensive and would require an engineering feat that would test mankind's engineering capabilities.

Another proposed solution was to increase the Earth's albedo effect.

Enhancing Earth's Albedo Effect - Albedo is the Latin word for "whiteness." White surfaces on the Earth, such as glaciers, ice caps, white clouds, and snow-covered land reflect a greater amount of incoming sunlight back into space versus darker surfaces. This results in less of the sun's energy being absorbed by Earth's surface and atmosphere, which has a cooling effect on the planet. To increase the albedo effect, scientists proposed placing large white reflective materials on unused lands to reflect sunlight back into space.

Ultimately, the committee tasked with making recommendations regarding the best and most practical climate geoengineering solutions to reverse global warming decided on a multi-pronged approach. They recommended all the carbon removal methods (ocean fertilization, carbon removal via filtering, and reforestation) and the construction of massive space-based mirrors to reflect 5% of sunlight heading towards Earth back into space to prevent the sunlight from reaching the Earth's atmosphere and surface.

Space-based mirrors were chosen over injections of aerosols because mirrors in space were a climate control method that scientists believed they could control more easily and precisely than injection of aerosols. They were concerned that if mankind injected aerosols into the Earth's atmosphere and it didn't work out as planned, the unintended consequences could be quite negative. If the injection of aerosols went awry, it could jeopardize the mission to block enough sunlight or conversely it could wind up blocking too much sunlight and cause an erratic and unstable climate. Whereas, space-based mirrors could be removed or added in order to precisely control the amount of sunlight reaching Earth, if adjustments were needed based on future observations.

The committee also recommended strict methane emission standards and implementing a method of methane removal from the atmosphere that involved injecting a chemical into the upper atmosphere that would react with methane and cause it to turn into carbon dioxide and water vapor. While not an ideal solution, methane is a far more potent global warming gas than carbon dioxide or water vapor and its accumulation in the atmosphere was troubling enough for scientists to recommend implementing measures to break it down into less potent carbon dioxide.

Unlike other international political squabbles, the effort to implement the engineering solutions recommended by the ICCMC went remarkably smoothly. The world community understood the importance of working together to solve the climate crisis. Mankind was once again proving that when their backs were against the wall, they were willing, ready, and able to come together to address a looming global crisis. It was a very hopeful moment for Scott and Sarah, as well as all other concerned inhabitants of Earth.

Part of the international agreement to implement the chosen engineering solutions was to implement them in the open for the entire world to see. This was agreed upon so the people of the Earth would have hope as they watched solutions to the climate crisis being implemented and because transparency and openness would add an important level of accountability that was needed for such large projects. The openness was also driven by a need to dispel conspiracy theorists and other cranks that would invariably question why the public couldn't witness the proposed solutions being implemented.

While adding iron to the oceans was not all that interesting since it just involved watching a war like armada of ships and planes dropping tiny iron pellets into the oceans throughout the world, Scott found the other solutions quite interesting to follow. Cameras were set up at key construction sites and a website was maintained that provided camera access and daily updates from the international body that was created to implement the engineering solutions, known as the International Climate Change Mitigation Agency (ICCMA).

Scott spent at least a few minutes each day viewing the ICCMA website to keep up with the progress taking place in desert areas, such as the southwestern United States, the Sahara Desert in North Africa, China's high desert plateau, and Australia's outback. Within six months, several small-scale prototypes of carbon dioxide filters were operating in these desert areas. To quickly develop the best carbon dioxide filter technology that could be implemented on a grand scale without delays; prototypes were built by a number of competing public-private efforts pitted against one another for a large cash prize.

ICCMA smartly took this competitive public-private approach to developing carbon dioxide filters to avoid having the development bogged down by top-heavy government management. Making it a competitive contest that private companies could participate in not only ensured quick results but also allowed various innovative approaches to be tried and evaluated simultaneously. It meant the ICCMA could quickly select the best concept to develop as a full-scale carbon dioxide filter, which was important since they needed to get the filters up and running as soon as possible.

It turned out that Tesla International wound up winning the cash prize and the contract to develop full-scale filters for placement in various locations throughout the world. For years prior to formation of the ICCMA, Tesla secretly worked on carbon dioxide filtering technology in anticipation of the day when it would be needed. Their anticipatory efforts paid off since their technology was far superior to other efforts. In fact, Tesla's filter technology, which used renewable energy to turn carbon dioxide removed from the air into usable bricks blew away the competition.

However, it wasn't a total loss for Tesla's competitors. Due to the enormous need for massive carbon dioxide filtering systems, the supply order could not possibly be filled by a single company as quickly as they were needed. Therefore, the ICCMA required Tesla to license its filter technology to several of the losing bidders and awarded the competitors each a percentage of the contracts to build the Tesla filters.

The space mirrors solution was performed as a massive public-private international construction effort. There was no point in having an economic or technological competition because of the price and scale of the mirrors and the technical difficulty of getting them set up in space above the Earth. Instead, the ICCMA sought the best minds throughout the world from both the public and private sectors to work together on the space mirrors solution under management of a committee of space agencies from several countries.

The space mirrors project proved to be more problematic than providing iron nutrients to help ocean algae bloom or developing massive carbon dioxide filtering systems. Not that the technologically was all that complicated. Humans knew how to build mirrors and they knew how to place man-made objects into orbit above the Earth. It was the massive scale and effort that was needed to install the enormous mirrors in space that was troubling the development team.

To be effective at reducing the global temperature, the mirrors needed to be large enough to reduce the amount of sunlight reaching the atmosphere and Earth's surface by 5%.

Initial concepts, which included massive ground-built mirror structures that would be sent into space by large rockets launched in unison were rejected as too risky and impractical. If one rocket failed to launch at exactly the same time as the others, the massive mirror structures would break apart.

Instead, engineers and project managers came up with a modular design in which supporting structures and small mirror segments would be brought into space and warehoused on manned space stations. Then, the structures would be constructed in space and the small mirror segments would be attached individually to the structures, as they were being built. This method had its own problems, as the number of workhours required to perform the work in space and the need for precise construction quality and mirror placement were costly and problematic for humans to perform.

The solution that engineers decided upon was to utilize hybrid robot/drones to perform the work. The robot/drones would fly the structural parts and mirrors from the space stations and construct a small section then return to the space stations to reload and set off to construct another small section. Robot and drone technology developed for prior space missions was easily customized to perform the necessary transportation and construction tasks as directed by human controllers located on the space stations.

The high-technology construction method proved very successful, and the mirrors were constructed quite efficiently once the initial kinks were worked out. However, the sheer size of the mirror building effort in space meant the mirrors wouldn't be fully operational until many years in the future, with an estimated completion date of 2085.

Chapter 16
A Sigh of Relief

By 2075, the carbon dioxide reducing geoengineering solutions had been fully implemented and humans around the world breathed a big sigh of relief while they waited to find out if the unprecedented geoengineering efforts would reduce the level of atmospheric carbon dioxide as predicted. Completion of the massive sunlight blocking mirror structures was still at least ten years away, but their construction was progressing as expected and people were optimistic that they'd be in full operation by 2085. Scott and Sarah were really feeling optimistic at this point. It seemed as if mankind had risen to the occasion and was on the road to recovery from the reckless way they had treated the Earth's atmosphere and environment.

The years that followed were encouraging, as carbon dioxide concentrations in the atmosphere started to slowly fall. However, due to the relatively high amount of carbon dioxide in the atmosphere, global temperatures, sea temperatures, and sea level continued to rise, albeit at a slower pace than during the recent past. The sense of optimism among humans was palpable, as the overheated planet was expected to start cooling as soon as the space-based mirrors became fully operational in 2085 and their cooling effect started to kick in.

Optimism continued during the late 2070s and early 2080s as the carbon dioxide reducing geoengineering solutions were operating smoothly, the space-based mirrors gradually became operational, and the intensity of sunlight reaching Earth slowly diminished towards the target level of a 5% reduction. The economic boom caused by the changeover to cheap, clean energy continued and was bolstered by the massive spending on geoengineering solutions. There was widespread hope that the geoengineering solutions that had been implemented with stunning success would ultimately save mankind from the worst aspects of global warming. The optimism that reigned led people to spend money on creature comforts and vacations, further boosting the world economy.

The sense of optimism was particularly high in 2082 as the ICCMA announced the space-based mirrors were 80% operational and on track for completion by 2085. At the same time, the Intergovernmental Panel on Climate Change (IPCC) reported that sunlight intensity had been reduced by 4% due to the space-based mirrors already in operation and they were expecting global temperatures to start dropping after 2085 when the space-based mirrors were fully operational.

While many people felt optimistic, as the masses believed the global warming problem had been solved, such optimism was not shared by everyone in the scientific community. Although the geoengineering solutions were having a real impact on the carbon dioxide level in the atmosphere and the intensity of sunlight reaching Earth, there were troubling signs in the polar regions of the planet that scientists were tracking. The polar regions had warmed significantly more than the mid-latitudes where most people lived and were experiencing the brunt of the warming that had occurred to date.

Chapter 17
Severe Turbulence

During 2083 the Earth's atmosphere continued to slowly warm and sea level continued to gradually rise, despite the slowly decreasing concentration of carbon dioxide in the atmosphere. The warming and sea level rise were due to the relatively high (yet decreasing) level of carbon dioxide in Earth's climate system and an increasing amount of atmospheric methane. While scientists were pleased about the carbon dioxide reductions, they were growing increasingly concerned about frozen methane (methane hydrate) releases from melting ice and tundra in the polar regions and from deposits beneath the oceans. It appeared methane was increasingly contributing to the ongoing warming and sea level rise.

A positive feedback loop had taken hold in which atmospheric warming caused melting of methane hydrate, which released methane gas into the atmosphere, which caused additional atmospheric warming. Once the Earth's climate enters a self-sustaining warming trend, the geologic record indicates it will continue until something significant occurs to stop and reverse it.

Before mankind existed, natural global warming caused by a positive feedback loop would eventually be reversed by an outside force that ended the warming trend and began a cooling trend. The outside force could include changes in the Earth's orbit that reduced the amount of sunlight reaching the Earth or rock weathering that removed carbon dioxide from the atmosphere and lessened the greenhouse effect.

Mankind tried to mimic a natural cooling force that could end the warming feedback loop by building the massive space-based mirror arrays, which were completed on time during the first few months of 2085. However, the cooling force of the reduced sunlight was not enough to overcome the warming force of methane hydrate's positive feedback loop that accelerated the release of the powerful global warming gas methane. As a result, the planet continued to warm despite the reduced amount of solar radiation reaching the surface and lower atmosphere thanks to the mirror arrays. This scenario in which methane gas became the primary driver of global warming was considered unlikely by scientists on the ICCMC when they chose the space mirrors option of reducing sunlight over an injection of aerosols. Unfortunately, despite the long odds, the unlikely scenario had turned into reality, as methane gas releases exceeded expectations and global warming continued despite the mirrors being fully operational.

By a vote of the United Nations, it was decided to expand the space-based mirrors to reduce sunlight reaching the Earth from 95% to 90%. However, the sheer size of the expansion effort meant it was no easy task, with estimates of 8 to 10 years for completion. Scientists and engineers assumed the expansion could be done more quickly than the time it took to install the original space-based mirror arrays given the knowledge gained from the initial installations, if all available resources were put to work to build and install the additional mirror arrays.

As work was desperately being performed to expand the space-based mirrors, the accelerated methane-caused warming problem was compounded by the ineffectiveness of the geoengineered solution that was implemented to reduce methane concentrations in the atmosphere. The chemical compound chosen by scientists that was expected to cause a reaction in which most of the methane high up in the atmosphere would be transformed into less potent carbon dioxide and water vapor proved largely ineffective for reasons that were not entirely understood. The most plausible explanation was the possibility that sunlight in the upper atmosphere was causing the chemical compound to break down before it could reach the targeted methane and cause the desired reaction that would have eliminated methane and its potent warming impact.

By 2086, methane emissions increased by a rate that sufficed to cause a faster rate of increase of global atmospheric and ocean temperatures. This caused melting of ice in the polar regions to speed up, which caused sea level to rise more quickly than it had in recent years. The positive feedback warming loop had kicked into a higher gear.

As people around the world fretted during 2086 about the increasing global warming trend linked to accelerating methane gas releases, a new crisis emerged. Nearly a third of the space-based mirrors were unexpectedly knocked offline as Earth was impacted by an unusually large barrage of meteors that took out many of the space-based mirrors, along with a number of satellites. The meteor shower was more focused and intense than what engineers had expected was possible when they designed the giant space mirror structures.

The destruction of nearly a third of the space-based mirrors by the unexpectedly large meteor shower increased the amount of sunlight impacting Earth to 97% of normal. This meant the mirrors were less effective at reducing global temperatures at a crucial time when they needed to be more effective due to the accelerated methane-caused warming.

The project to add additional space-based mirrors was in full swing when the meteor shower hit. It had to be suspended as a damage assessment was needed to determine how the large mirror arrays could be reconstructed and expanded given the damage they had suffered. The best estimates were 11 years for installation of enough mirror structures to reduce sunlight to 90% of normal, which meant the mirrors wouldn't be fully operational until at least 2097.

People with awareness of the increasingly dire situation were collectively holding their breath hoping the space-based mirrors could be rebuilt faster than anticipated. However, the lack of mirrors was only half of the problem. The problem of increasing methane accumulation in the atmosphere also had to be addressed.

Scientists and knowledgeable people understood that if left unchecked methane releases had a real potential to cause runaway global warming since there was so much frozen methane hydrate in the polar regions and beneath the ocean floors. If a tremendous amount of methane was liberated from its long-frozen state and ejected into the atmosphere, it would cause a significant global temperature rise that would have catastrophic consequences for all living things on Earth.

With carbon dioxide reduction methods working, it had now become clear to the scientific community that methane was the primary concern that had to be addressed immediately to head off catastrophic global warming. The space-based mirrors would eventually bring temperatures down once completed, but the more immediate concern was keeping temperatures from rising any further by removing methane from the atmosphere.

Given the dire circumstance, implementing an enormous project to inject aerosols into the atmosphere to quickly reduce sunlight intensity was an option that was under consideration. But it would require at least five years to fully implement and carried a number of risks, some of which were in the unknown category which made scientists and world leaders nervous about trying this method of sunlight reduction. Ultimately, world leaders decided against pursuing massive aerosols injections.

Leaving nothing to chance, in late 2086 the ICCMA sprung back into action. The agency still existed as a shell of its former greatness. Its main function since 2075 had been to support maintenance efforts for the geoengineered solutions they put into place and to continue researching new more effective solutions.

Governments, industry, and wealthy individuals around the world combined forces to ensure the ICCMA was well funded, as there was a foreboding feeling throughout humanity that the ICCMA had to find a solution to the methane problem and find it quickly. The agency spent the early part of 2087 hiring scientists and setting up facilities to test proposed chemical compounds capable of addressing the methane accumulation problem in a desperate effort to stop the positive feedback loop that threatened to send global warming into a catastrophic runaway phase. There was growing concern that the warming would eventually increase so rapidly that there would be no way to stop it by any human means.

Chapter 18
Crossing the Event Horizon

By late 2087, it became obvious the ICCMA was not making any progress in finding the silver bullet chemical compound that humans needed to reduce methane in the atmosphere to head off catastrophic global warming. The agency was bogged down testing compounds in small amounts in the upper atmosphere using specially designed drones. They could not afford to make the same mistake they had made previously and approve a compound that was ineffective at destroying methane in the upper atmosphere. Unfortunately, the compounds they tested broke down too quickly in the harsh conditions of the upper atmosphere and so far proved to be ineffective. The desperately needed breakthrough was elusive.

Despite the best efforts of the team in charge, the space-based mirror project was behind schedule due to unforeseen shortages of materials and problems integrating the partially destroyed mirror arrays with the new structures and mirrors being attached. The completion date was pushed back to 2105.

The climate crisis grew dire as the year turned to 2088. Methane releases in polar regions and from beneath the oceans continued to accelerate and were making travel by boat dangerous in some parts of the world. A ship that passed over a massive methane gas vent in the Gulf of Alaska sank, as its buoyancy was affected by the bubbling greenhouse gas rising from the ocean floor below.

Ships started reporting huge fire columns emanating from methane-rich ocean areas, as static electricity and lightning caused methane escaping from the oceans to catch fire. Scientists warned that it was only a matter of time before methane-caused fire columns occurred close enough to land to affect humans and set off massive forest fires.

The start of 2089 brought humanity even more troubling news. The carbon dioxide level in the atmosphere started increasing. The increase was caused by massive forest and bush fires that released carbon dioxide in large quantities and an uptick in the release of carbon dioxide from ice sheets and tundra in polar regions that melted at a faster pace than the recent past. The release of carbon dioxide into the atmosphere was so significant that the geoengineering solutions designed to remove the greenhouse gas were overwhelmed and rendered ineffective.

During the 2090s, Earth's atmosphere warmed at the unthinkable rate of approximately 1.0 degree Celsius (1.8 degrees Fahrenheit) per decade. This rate of increase was so fast that it was making adaption and survival a challenge for many species on Earth, including Homo sapiens. Water supplies dwindled in many areas and crops failed to grow as farmable areas suffered from severe heat and drought. As the decade wore on, farmlands started to transform into arid desert environments.

Humans had survived many natural climate changes in the past. In fact, our ancient human ancestors had survived several ice ages and warm interglacial periods prior to human civilization taking hold around 3200 BC. However, the climate change humans endured during the late 21st century was far faster than anything our ancestors had adapted to previously. Past natural climate changes from ice ages to warm interglacial periods took thousands of years for a similar temperature increase of 1 degree Celsius (1.8 degrees Fahrenheit) to occur, allowing plenty of time for humans to adapt to their changing climate.

As the 21st century drew to a close, another major collapse of ice sheets occurred in both Greenland and the Antarctic, which raised sea level by an additional 10 meters (33 feet) within just a few weeks, with no end to the sea level rise in sight since the Earth's oceans and atmosphere were warming rapidly.

Coastal flood protections around the world were overrun with water. Humans had simply not prepared for such a substantial sea-level rise of 10 meters (33 feet) within a period of only a few weeks. The massive flooding that ensued killed many millions of people who couldn't evacuate low-lying coastal areas quickly enough and left billions of people without a home or a place to work. The flooding also took out numerous Earth-based support facilities that supplied materials to the space stations used by the space-based mirror construction project, causing further delays to the already behind schedule project. The completion date was uncertain but was now estimated as the year 2110.

Chapter 19

Reflections

By the turn of the century in 2100 it had become clear that the Earth was undergoing a climate catastrophe that had morphed into self-sustaining runaway global warming that humans were losing the ability to control.

As runaway global warming took hold in the new century and human civilization started showing signs of cracking, Scott convinced Sarah to move back to the area where he grew up in the remote Yukon. They had saved a stash of gold coins over the years to help them during hard times and were prepared to leave their jobs and live independently. Scott felt they would be best off living in a remote area since climate change was obviously no longer just a crisis and had morphed into a world-wide disaster with an uncertain outcome. The last thing he wanted was for them to live their later years in an urban area like Calgary relying on others to survive and exposing themselves to the plethora of diseases that the warming planet had unleashed upon humanity.

There was already a stream of climate refugees that had made their way into Calgary from the United States and

Mexico. He assumed this migration would only grow over time as the climate to the south grew more inhospitable making the city more crowded and dangerous.

Scott had a sinking feeling as he and Sarah prepared to leave Calgary for the great white north of the Yukon that civilization itself was crumbling and may cease to exist. It was such an odd thing for him to consider. It was not all that long ago that mankind seemed to be the master of the universe. Just a few years ago plans were in the works to populate Mars, many mundane tasks had been taken over by robots, most diseases and debilitating health conditions had been conquered, and life expectancy had reached heights never attained before in human history. He realized that it was all only a facade. Without a stable climate and livable environment, human civilization and human survival as a species were just as fragile as any ecosystem on Earth.

As they ate one of their last dinners at their apartment in Calgary, Sarah said with concern in her voice, "I'm worried about leaving Calgary. Things are getting bad, but at least we still have the necessities of modern life. I am afraid of the unknown in the Yukon."

Scott replied in a confident voice, "We have a better chance surviving in the sparsely populated Yukon where I grew up, living off the land, than relying on others and trying to survive the growing chaos in Calgary. Who knows what this is leading to? Look at how quickly things have gone from normal to the growing chaos we are experiencing here."

She grabbed hold of his hand and said in a halting voice, "I'm just afraid Scott."

Scott rubbed her hand gently and with confidence said, "Trust me Sarah. Just as I trusted you that week we met all those years ago in California when you led me away from the dangerous fire to a safe haven in front of the hotel."

She smiled at the memory from so long ago and nodded. They held hands in silence a few minutes longer until she broke the silence and said, "I trust you Scott. I know what we need to do. I just needed reassurance that we are doing the right thing."

Within a week they left their apartment in Calgary and made their way north towards the Yukon, knowing they'd probably never again see the city they called home for so many years.

On their trek north, while Sarah looked out of the window at the changing scenery, Scott reminisced about spending time with his grandfather as a child in the Yukon and the countless hours that papa Joe spent debating and debunking global warming with anyone who cared to listen. Calling it nothing more than an elaborate international conspiracy designed to scare people into submission to world government and to feed green industries and paper-pushing scientists. Scott shook his head and scoffed to himself thinking back to those days. "What folly papa Joe's crusade against addressing global warming turned out to be," Scott thought. He then laughed in a hopeless way.

Sarah, who was beleaguered and very concerned about their future, shot Scott a look and asked sternly, "What could possibly be funny at this moment, Scott?"

Scott was a bit shocked by her reaction and replied, "Oh, I wasn't actually laughing in a funny way. I was thinking of my grandfather. You know, papa Joe that I've talked about?"

Sarah nodded.

He continued, "I laughed at the utter absurdity of how he thought global warming was a hoax and had all sorts of conspiracies to back up his dismissive position. My grandfather's crusade against anyone who thought global warming was a problem we should address just seems so absurd now that we and humanity as a whole are facing an increasingly serious climate catastrophe. I mean look at us, we've left our home in Calgary, a modern city that is falling apart, and we're heading to the remote Yukon to survive. The thought just made me laugh out of disgust at our predicament that my grandfather and many of his generation unfortunately thought was a hoax and failed to address."

Sarah put her arm on Scott's shoulders to soothe him as he drove their electric SUV northward into the increasingly wild Canadian northlands. Feeling her arm on his shoulders brought him back to the night decades ago when they were trying to figure how to escape the wildfire that was raging outside of their hotel in California and Sarah put her arms around him for the first time to comfort him. He turned his head, looked at her and smiled. She knew that he was thinking back to their first embrace and smiled back.

They spent the night near Whitehorse, camping out on the outskirts of the small city. The next morning, they picked up some additional supplies in the city before continuing northward. Scott's memory was jarred as they drove past the vircade where he used to stop as a child to play VR games. As they drove past, he thought, "Still there? It's like I'm living in the Climate Crash game now."

Scott switched on the SUV's radio to pass the time as they drove northward. Instead of being greeted by music, the station was airing a special news segment. The announcer stated, "The government has activated the Canadian National Guard, as it appears American troops are amassing on the border. The long-feared American annexation of Canada appears imminent, as America's breadbasket has run dry and they appear ready to seize Canada's prairies and farmlands."

He quickly turned off the radio. It was the last thing he needed to hear at this moment.

After driving for a couple of hours, their electric SUV indicated it needed a charge. As he pulled up to a charging station at a rest area, a shot rang out. They were both startled and looked to the right where the shot originated from a wooded area.

A ragged man ran to the edge of the woods about fifty meters from them and told them in no uncertain terms to keep moving. He yelled, "I don't want to get any of your city folk's diseases! If you know what's good for you, keep moving!"

They promptly complied.

Luckily, it was late morning and there was plenty of sunlight left, so Scott found a sunny spot hidden from the main road and set up his solar charger to recharge the SUV's battery.

"We might as well have some lunch," he said to Sarah.

They set up a nice picnic spread in the warm sun next to a bubbling brook with a beautiful mountain view to look at.

As she took in a breath of the fresh Yukon air, Sarah said with a bit of alarm in her voice and wide-open eyes, "What the hell was that?"

Scott replied, "I don't know. The guy was either crazy or more likely a survivalist who decided his best chance of surviving was to avoid other humans."

Sarah replied, "I hope we don't wind up like that guy!"

They shared a laugh at the thought of it.

It all seemed surreal to Scott and Sarah to be sharing a picnic on such a beautiful sunny day, the kind of day that made them feel so good to be alive on Earth, knowing the human race faced such an uncertain future.

They made it to the small settlement in the remote part of the Yukon where Scott grew up. It was deserted. His family home was still there but was quite worn by the elements. It appeared nobody had lived there for a number of years.

He said to Sarah with a sarcastic tone, "Home, sweet home!"

She smiled and said, "We'll just have to make do."

He said, "My papa Joe may have been a strong-headed guy who was set in his ways, but thankfully he taught me how to survive in the woods. I will always be grateful to him for taking the time to teach me his survival skills."

She responded, "Do you think you remember it all?"

He replied, "It's like riding a bike, you never forget these things. Plus, I've kept my survival skills sharp with the extreme camping club I was in for years. I told you how rough those weekends were. We literally hiked into the woods with minimal provisions and put our survival skills to work to survive under different scenarios. It was fun for those of us from remote parts that found ourselves in Calgary to get out to the back country and survive off the land. I learned more from those people than I did from papa Joe, although he gave me a great foundation on which to build."

He took a breath, contemplated a bit and then continued, "Besides, Whitehorse is only four hours away and we have an electric SUV with a solar charger. We also have a healthy amount of money and gold coins. We won't be spending any of it here. We can get supplies from Whitehorse if we need them. One thing we need to do immediately is covering the road that leads here at the point where it breaks off from the main road with brush and fallen trees. We don't want any unexpected visitors."

Sarah shuddered at the thought of living so remotely but trusted that they had made the right decision to leave Calgary for the northern woods. It wasn't as if they had anything to look forward to Calgary, which seemed to be spiraling towards anarchy when they departed.

They lived several good years in the remoteness of the Yukon. While Sarah missed human interaction, she grew to love the resourcefulness that Scott taught her. She was amazed that they could actually live off the land after living with so many comforts in a city for decades. Scott taught her how to hunt animals using a crossbow, how to forage for berries and other edible plants, and even how to construct a shelter using trees and dirt.

One night they were lying in bed and started talking about their predicament. One of Scott's hobbies was monitoring his Ham radio to find out what was going on in the world. He let her know the situation in Calgary had grown desperate as the population experienced a rapid decline due to food shortages, deadly disease epidemics, and social disorder. It seemed as if cities would soon be uninhabitable as public services and the traditional economy were disappearing as the population disappeared.

He also revealed that the last hope for reversal of the rapid global warming trend, the space-based mirror project, had been abandoned in 2102 after the massive sea level rise at the turn of the century and the chaos that ensued in the world afterward. The people working for the agency overseeing the project abandoned their posts as many of their worksites flooded and civilization crumbled into chaos.

Sarah said in a tired voice, "I'm glad I trusted your judgment Scott when you told me it was time to move out."

He looked over, stroked her forehead and said, "It's sad what's become of our world. It's like human beings are devolving back to the hunter-gatherers they were before civilization began. I'm surprised at how quickly things have unraveled. I'm just glad I'm spending these years with you, my soul mate in this thing we call life."

She blushed, gave him a kiss, and said goodnight.

Scott had a strange dream before he woke up. Papa Joe visited him in the dream along with another couple he recognized but wasn't sure who they were. They were all consoling him and telling him everything would be okay.

The dream seemed to last a long time when he suddenly woke up in a hot sweat and looked over at Sarah. She was face down in her pillow. He thought she was just sleeping deeply and put his hand gently on her shoulder. It was cold. He was shocked. He knew right away that she had passed away in her sleep. Now he understood the couple in his dream was her parents, apparently there to console him about what he awoke to.

With a heavy heart, he lay there in shock listening to the rain beat down on the roof as it brightened outside. There was nobody to tell of her passing. It was now just him alone in the remote Yukon woods.

Once the rain cleared, he gained his composure and gave Sarah a proper burial in the area where his relatives had been laid to rest on the edge of the settlement. It was an emotional farewell that he had to endure on his own. He took comfort knowing the spirits of papa Joe and her parents had visited him the night before and were there with him to share this moment at his time of need.

Chapter 20
Peering into Eternity

As a Ham radio enthusiast, Scott monitored the disturbing chain of events in which human civilization bent, then broke and unraveled because of the pressure applied by runaway global warming. Regular means of communication over long distances had disappeared as societies across the globe suffered breakdowns. However, just as they had done in the past during natural disasters that destroyed regular communication systems, amateur radio operators using high frequency Ham radios kept the lines of communication open across the globe as the climate disaster wiped out other methods of communication.

It was eerie for Scott to be witness to humanity's final calamity from the safe remote reaches of the Yukon Territory. He kept a journal of the events he heard unfold over his radio in part to help keep his mind sharp and in part hoping if humans did somehow survive this ordeal, someone someday might find his written record of the tragic events that were occurring.

Since Sarah passed away, he no longer took trips to Whitehorse. It wouldn't be worth it, anyway. There was hardly anyone left in the small Yukon city the last time he visited it with his late wife. He assumed it was a ghost town now.

It was quite invigorating for Scott as an older man to be back in nature surviving on his own, but also odd to be back living where he grew up; the only person inhabiting the once bustling settlement.

He spent a lot of time during the summer of 2107 talking to an isolated survivalist Ham radio operator that lived in central Alaska who went by the handle Jinko. His Alaskan radio acquaintance informed him that civilization as they had known it had crumbled and humans were, as far as he could tell, going extinct.

Jinko passed on disturbing stories of massive crop failures and starvation, as humans couldn't adjust their farming practices to the rapid global warming that was now occurring. Food supplies were also heavily impacted by the fact that low-lying farmlands had been flooded by sea level that was approximately 42 meters (138 feet) higher than where they were 100 years ago.

He also passed along horrific stories about disease pandemics sweeping across the world that were decimating mankind. The breakdown of civilization resulted in the release of disease-causing biological agents from military bio-warfare research facilities around the world.

Additionally, ancient viruses that had been frozen in tundra and polar ice for millions of years were released by the melting tundra and ice, exposing humans to viruses they had never encountered. With modern medicines and medical treatment no longer available and no natural immunity to these previously unencountered diseases, exposed humans had terrible survival odds.

Although Scott had grown to like and trust Jinko, he naturally needed to confirm his Ham radio buddy's dire reports since they were so disturbing and serious. He spent a good part of late 2107 and early 2108 contacting other ham radio operators around the world. Unfortunately, he confirmed that Jinko was not exaggerating or making things up. Other ham radio operators confirmed that things had grown very dire for mankind, with most countries throughout the world completely depopulated as their ability to grow food had been destroyed by the desertification of farmlands due to the warming atmosphere. Those who scrounged for food and were able to survive for a time were wiped out by endless waves of diseases. The rapidly warming climate severely weakened human's immune systems, making them unable to fight off wave after wave of disease pandemics. Humans had given up on trying to reproduce, as all their energy was used to find scarce food and to try to survive the endless parade of diseases in vain. His radio contacts confirmed that humans were going extinct.

Over time, he lost contact with the ham radio operators that he had been checking in with over the years. They were all survivalists, some of whom were doing their survivalist thing close to cities. The message Scott received from them was clear. The population of the world was gone. All that remained was a few aging and isolated survivalists like themselves, who were too old to have children. One by one, their radios went silent as they too succumbed to the ravages of runaway global warming and the perils of old age.

His last contact with another human was with his radio friend Jinko during 2111. Like him, Jinko had avoided the deadly pandemics that had swept across the planet since they both lived remotely without physical contact with other human beings.

In June 2111 he spoke to Jinko, who informed Scott that he felt his time had come, as his heart was failing. Despite his best efforts, Scott couldn't raise Jinko on the radio during July. He knew Jinko wouldn't ignore his radio calls and sensed he had passed away alone in the woods as he wanted to pass.

He got up from his radio table and walked to the porch on the front of his house, sat down, and gazed out at the sunset that was just starting over the hills to the west. It was a clear warm summer evening. The sound of leaves gently rustling in the warm breeze was the only sound that greeted him.

As he sat there looking at the increasingly colorful sunset, he thought about all that had transpired during his life, much of it with papa Joe in the very hills and valleys he was looking out at as the sunset filled the sky with brilliant colors. The bright planet Venus was the only celestial body visible to Scott as the sunlight waned; an extremely hot planet that had long ago undergone natural runaway global warming that transformed the formerly temperate water-laden planet into an inhospitably hot and waterless place.

As the dwindling sunlight faded into the hills and a small group of caribou crossed through the empty settlement, Scott started having a sinking feeling that when he eventually dies, he will take the last human breath on Earth. A species done in by natural forces it had unleashed on the planet it had inhabited for hundreds of thousands of years. Natural forces that it as a species did not respect enough to live with in harmony. Natural forces that ran wild because of the excesses that had once been human civilization; excesses that were counteracted severely by the natural world and would soon render Homo sapiens an extinct species.

Research Resources

To learn more about global warming and climate change, the following are some recommended resources.

- Environment and Climate Change Canada – climate.weather.gc.ca

- U.S. Government Climate Statistics – Climate.gov

- Mauna Loa Observatory CO2 Readings – www.esrl.noaa.gov/gmd/ccgg/trends/

- Climate Statistics Updates to Storms of My Grandchildren – www.columbia.edu/~mhs119/

- Climate Central – climatecentral.org

- Real Climate – realclimate.org

- Skeptical Science – skepticalscience.com

About the Author

With guidance from his mother who had a keen interest in science and reading, John Coviello started following the global warming saga in the late 1970s, long before it was widely known as a potential problem or even showed up as a strong signal in the global climate records. Embracing a lifelong interest in the environment in which we live, John earned a degree in Environmental Science. He worked in the field of environmental science for approximately twenty years and has followed environmental issues with a passion. His other passions are writing and observing the weather.

I hope you enjoyed this book and found it worthwhile to read. If you would like to be placed on a mailing list, so you will be made aware of future books by John Coviello, send an email to: ROKENT20@gmail.com.